*TI...*
*ENOUGH*
*FOR*
*DRUMS*

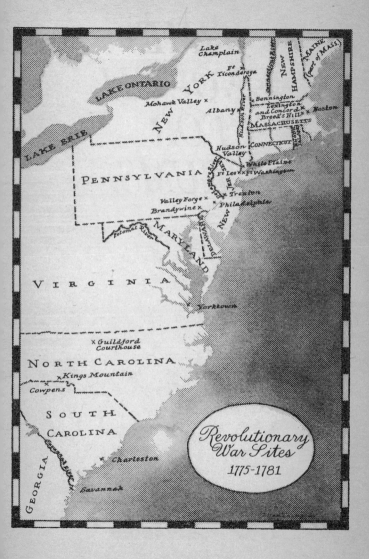

Lake Champlain

Ft Ticonderoga

LAKE ONTARIO

NEW YORK

NEW HAMPSHIRE

MAINE (part of Mass.)

Mohawk Valley ×

Albany ×

Bennington ×

Lexington and Concord ×

Breed's Hill ×

Boston ×

MASSACHUSETTS

LAKE ERIE

Hudson Valley

CONNECTICUT

White Plains ×

PENNSYLVANIA

Ft Lee ×

× Ft Washington

NEW JERSEY

× Trenton

Valley Forge ×

× Philadelphia

Brandywine ×

Potomac River

MARYLAND

DELAWARE

VIRGINIA

× Yorktown

× Guildford Courthouse

NORTH CAROLINA

× Kings Mountain

× Cowpens

SOUTH CAROLINA

GEORGIA

Savannah River

× Charleston

Savannah

*Revolutionary War Sites 1775-1781*

# ANN RINALDI

# *TIME ENOUGH FOR DRUMS*

**Troll Associates**

A TROLL BOOK, published by Troll Associates,
Mahwah, NJ 07430

Published by arrangement with Holiday House, Inc. For information
address Holiday House, Inc., 18 East 53rd Street, New York,
New York 10010.

First Troll Printing, 1988

Printed in the United States of America.

10  9  8  7  6  5  4  3  2  1

ISBN 0-8167-1269-7

For my son, RON,
a twentieth-century Patriot
who opened my eyes to my country's history

# TIME
# ENOUGH
# FOR
# DRUMS

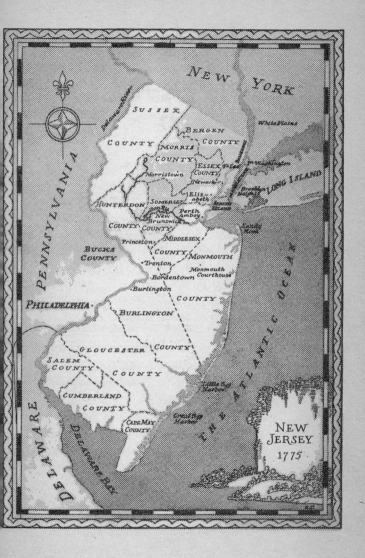

# CHAPTER

*1*

The cold wind stung my face and brought tears to my eyes when I turned into it to look at my brother Dan, who stood next to me on the hill. It seemed like all of Trenton was laid out below us in grays and browns with nothing to recommend it on that cheerless December day. But what we saw was only King and Queen Streets as we stood on the rise where they converged.

"Are you ready, Jem?"

"Yes."

He handed the musket to me. I could not believe it was so heavy, and for a second I almost dropped it, but then I grabbed it with both hands.

Dan smiled. "Twelve pounds. You sure you still want to do this?"

"You know I do. Don't tease. Let's do it before someone sees us. I'm freezing."

"All right, then, here." He took his cartridge box from his shoulder and draped it over me. "You won't be wearing one, of course, but you should always have cartridges made up at the house. I showed you how to do that."

We'd done it one night when our parents had been out. Dan had been rolling cartridges at the kitchen table, and I'd gotten him to show me how. I'd even rolled some.

"Now hold the musket hip-height or whatever way is comfortable for you to load. All right?"

"Like this?"

"That's fine. Next, take the cartridge out of the box and tear it apart with your teeth. Go ahead, put it between your teeth. That's right. You know, a soldier can be deficient in many ways, Jem, but he's got to have at least two good teeth."

I ripped the end off the paper cartridge and spat it out. If only I weren't so cold. If only I could stop shaking. If only the gun weren't so heavy.

"There's powder in there now and a musket ball, as you know. So pour some of the powder into the pan. That's it. That's enough. Close the hammer. . . ."

I did.

"Now pour the rest of the powder and the musket ball and the paper wadding into the barrel. Careful. That's it. Take the ramrod out. Here . . . *This* is the ramrod . . . I've *told* you, Jem!"

"Daniel Emerson, you may have done this *hundreds* of times. . . ."

"You're doing fine, Jem. No girl I know in town would even hold a musket."

I wasn't doing fine. The musket was too heavy. I couldn't keep it all straight in my head, but I would do it. I was determined.

"Now, full-cock the cock. That's it."

"I . . . can't . . . get . . . it . . . all . . . the . . . way . . . back."

"Yes, you can. There you go. You've got it. Bring it up to your shoulder so you can fire. No, Jem, not *on* your shoulder, *against* it. You've got to brace it. There, that's it. Pull the trigger. Go ahead."

I tried. It wouldn't go back at first, but Dan was coaxing. "Steady, hold your feet firm on the ground. Do it, Jem!" I fired.

The world exploded. The impact almost knocked me over, but Dan steadied me. The noise was deafening. For a moment I couldn't hear, couldn't think, and I could almost taste the black powder in my mouth. But I had fired!

Dan took the musket, smiling. "You did fine. But you'll have to go through the moves a little faster. Do you think you can remember all you have to do?"

"How can she? She can't even remember to come for her lessons when her tutor is waiting for her."

He said it plain and quiet, but there, just near the row of trees, was John Reid, my tutor, on his horse. Dan and I turned to stare, speechless. Where had he come from? There had been no one around a moment before. We watched, as if under a spell, as John Reid got off his horse and came toward us.

"I wish you were as attentive with your French, Jemima. I ought to give musket-firing lessons. Then I wouldn't have to leave a warm fire and hunt you down."

"I'm sorry, John," Dan said. "I didn't know Jem had lessons this afternoon."

"Lessons are every Monday, Wednesday, and Friday afternoon." Reid was looking at me, not my brother, as he spoke. His brown eyes bored into me. "You haven't been home that much, Daniel, so you wouldn't know."

"Jem said—"

"Jem lied. A practice she's been known to indulge in to get her own way."

"John, I don't think Jem would—"

"Yes, she would." Reid turned his steadfast gaze from me to Dan. "She resorts to every sort of trickery she can think of to get out of lessons. And to provoke me. I'm quite used to it. It's been going on for two years now. But this..."

He stared at the polished and gleaming musket in Dan's hands. Then he sighed and looked from one of us to the other. "I trust your parents know about this."

"No, John," Dan said, "they don't." His words carried all the meaning they needed. Their eyes met. They were friends. Reid was four years older than Dan, but his authority over me made those four years seem like ten.

The wind gusted. I drew my blanket coat around me. Reid's rough brown cloak billowed, making him look imposing and sinister.

"I trust you had good reason for this, then."

"You know I leave in a month, John. With the war coming..." Now Dan sighed. "In my travels around the county I found many of the menfolk teaching the women to use weapons."

Reid nodded. "Ah yes, the war. Damned nuisance. It's all my boys talk about at school. It's putting strange ideas into the young people's heads. You know that your brother David is off at the steel mill with John Fitch again this afternoon when he's supposed to be at his apprenticeship with John Singer."

"No, I didn't," Dan said. "What do they do at the mill?"

"Make gunlocks for the American army."

"Gunlocks?"

"Yes, gunlocks." Reid's boots crunched on the frozen ground as he strode back to his horse. "Which isn't what Fitch is supposed to be doing there, but what he does nevertheless. And David with him. It seems I spend half my time these days tracking down your errant brother and sister."

"I'll fetch David as soon as I leave here," Dan promised.

"I'd appreciate that. And if it makes you feel any better, I'd probably teach my sister to use a musket, too, if I had a sister. After I birched her first for lying." He got on his horse and sat, considering us.

"I'll say nothing to your parents about this. It would only worry them needlessly."

"Thank you, John."

"I wasn't lying, Mr. Reid." I looked at him.

His eyes softened into familiar mockery. "We'll discuss it Friday at lessons, Jemima."

"I wasn't. Dan and I were to meet here a full hour before lessons. But he was late. And I lost all sense of time."

"She's speaking the truth," Dan said. "I was at the Moores' and left poor Jem here freezing in the cold."

"All right, Jemima. I'll let you off this time. But you'd better concoct some tale to tell your mother. She knows you missed your schoolwork today. Lying shouldn't be too difficult for you. You're telling tales all the time."

He veered his horse toward town, leaving me with the sting of his unkind words. I watched his retreating figure and wondered if he would indeed keep this musket lesson a secret from our parents. And how he knew that John Fitch was making gunlocks at the steel mill. And why it mattered that he had hurt me when I considered him so despicable.

# CHAPTER

## 2

I had an errand to run after leaving Dan, so I hurried along Queen Street. Mrs. Pinkerton was ailing and Mother said I was to deliver a copy of *Gulliver's Travels* for her to read. I delivered the book to David Pinkerton's shop, inquired after his wife's health, took quick note of the price of his printed calicoes, as Father had asked me to do, and then looked to see if he was still stocking tea.

He was. My father was a merchant too and hadn't sold tea in his shop since early 1774 when Dan and the other students at the College of New Jersey in Princeton had burned the school's supply in protest of the tax on tea the British had imposed on us back in 1773. I went back out into the cold, thinking of how dearly the decision not to carry tea must have cost Father. Many people patronized Pinkerton's shop now instead, and my father had a lot of other difficulties, too. Since October he'd been a member of the Committee of Safety, which meant he had a say not only in the commissioning of military officers for our army but also in how the money should be spent that the legislature issued. And he had to keep an eye on the activities of avowed Tories, those who were loyal to the king, in our town. And many of them were his friends.

"Jemima. Jemima Emerson!"

Up ahead a figure came running toward me. I recognized Raymond Moore instantly in his round, flat-brimmed Quaker hat and somber clothes. The Moore farm, where Dan had been earlier, was two miles outside town. Raymond was the younger of the two sons and always my favorite. We'd played together as children, Dan, David, and I and the Moore children. But in the last year or so, he'd been looking at me with different eyes. I must say his looks quickened my heart, though I was determined it would be a long time before I married.

His parents and mine were friends, in the steadfast but inscrutable way Quakers were friends with people. Dan was just about betrothed to Raymond's sister, Betsy.

"Hello, Jemima."

"You would think the devil himself was chasing you, Raymond."

He stood holding his hat in both hands against his heaving chest. The Moores grew their corn and their sons tall, Father always said. He'd forgotten to add handsome. But Raymond's handsomeness was obscured by some private anguish.

"I would speak with thee."

"Fine, you can walk me home."

"No. Here. We mustn't let thy parents see us together."

"Why? Do we have some secret they wouldn't approve of?"

"Don't jest. In fact, perhaps we soon shall if I persist in my plan."

"And what plan is that?"

"My plan to enlist in thy brother's regiment."

"Oh, Raymond!" I stopped dead in my shoes. Our eyes met, and in his I saw all the pain and determination of his decision. "Why, Raymond? I don't want you to go away and fight. Isn't it enough that Dan is going? And perhaps David too? And almost everyone I know?"

"I have seen thy brother running himself ragged these last six weeks to recruit men for the company he's had to raise to prove himself worthy of his commission. I have watched and stood by in silence while others I grew up with have signed on. And I know he hasn't reached his quota of men yet. Betsy has told me."

"Has Betsy also told you what it will do to your parents if you enlist?"

"She's not had to tell me that. I have anguished and prayed on my decision. Thy brother and I have been close for many years. I cannot stay and let him fight the British so we can keep our land."

"But it's against your faith to fight."

"It is of the Quaker philosophy that if thee has a concern, thee has the responsibility to follow through on it. I have a concern."

He looked at me, waiting. I was cold through to the bone and anxious about the trouble I was in at home. I was annoyed with Raymond, who had suddenly become very dear to me as he stood there talking about Quaker philosophy.

"I'll never forgive you if you get killed. Do you know that?"

He smiled. "Thee will help me, then?"

"How can I help?"

He cast glances up and down Queen Street, which was deserted. "Will Dan be home tonight?"

"He comes and goes as he pleases these days. Sometimes

when he's out recruiting, he doesn't come home until morning. And sometimes young men knock on our door in the middle of the night to enlist. He did promise Mother he'd be home for supper, though. We're having Indian pot roast. He wouldn't miss that."

"I will be in thy barn at ten tonight. All thee has to do is tell Dan. It would anguish thy parents if I came to the house."

"Oh, Raymond!"

"It disturbs thee."

"Yes, it disturbs me. I know the Patriot women are supposed to send their men off to war with pride. And I am proud. But it still disturbs me. And what will Betsy say about Dan taking you? He's about to ask for her hand, you know."

"Betsy knows I will enlist elsewhere if not with Dan."

The wind gusted around us, wrapping us both in guilt and misery. "All right," I agreed. "I'll tell Dan." His eyes sought mine as he lingered. He started to speak, then stopped.

"Yes, Raymond?"

"I hold thee in very high esteem, Jemima Emerson. I'll not forget thee." He turned and ran, leaving me with my mouth open in the middle of the street.

# CHAPTER
## 3

Dan did come home that night as he had promised, but the chance to tell him about Raymond Moore was lost because of the presence of John Reid at our table.

Reid was a weasel if there ever was one. He bullied me in my lessons, scolded me constantly about my penmanship, and was not "agreeable to the newest rules and truest methods practiced by the best teachers," as he advertised in the *Pennsylvania Gazette* for his boys' school in Trenton.

And he was a Tory, reason alone for me to hate him. I'd heard that he birched the boys in his school when they misbehaved. If it was true, it added a menacing quality to him, which he did nothing to dispel.

Mother said nothing about my misadventures that day. She was too busy supervising Lucy in the kitchen. She sent me to the parlor to fetch both Reid and Dan for supper. In the hall I met David, freshly scrubbed and dressed. David was fourteen and at the moment very sullen.

"That Reid is a rat."

"What did he do, David?"

"Told Father I was with Fitch again today."

"What did Father do?"

"Nothing yet. Hasn't said a word to me about it."

That was worse than anything. Father was slow to anger, but when he did, he demanded intellectual argument. You had to defend yourself, and he didn't back off until you were in tears.

"Reid sent Dan for me, that's what he did."

"Did Dan scold?"

"No. Dan understands what I'm trying to do with Fitch. All he said was to be careful. Then I got back here and found that Reid had told Father. Who does he think he is, a member of this family?"

"Mother and Father have practically adopted him, you know that, David. We just have to put up with him."

"You, maybe. But I don't. I tell you, he's a rat."

"A weasel was more what I had in mind." I kissed the side of his face. He was taller than I, even though I was fifteen that December of 1775. I would be sixteen in March. "Just be good at supper. Maybe Father will forget it."

"Some chance."

I found Dan and Reid in front of the hearth in the parlor, each with a mug in his hand, conspiring. Then Dan gave a hearty laugh. The firelight slanted their shadows across the room.

John Reid was twenty-four, and I would be lying if I said he wasn't handsome. He was finely dressed in rust-colored breeches and coat with a lace cravat at his throat. His parents were dead. They had drowned at sea when their ship went down on a trip to England three years ago. His father and mine had been boyhood friends. His inheritance had allowed him to open his school for boys on King Street. He lived alone above the establishment, as befitted a weasel.

Dan was twenty, as tall as Reid but broader and more

direct in manner. He wore boots and immaculate linen breeches, shirt, and waistcoat. The blue and red coat of his regiment, the Second New Jersey, lay over a chair. He wore it not to affect a uniform, but because no other coat fit him since he'd come home from school.

"Dan, Mother says you're to come in to supper immediately. You too, Mr. Reid."

"How nice you look, Jem. Doesn't she look pretty, John?"

Reid inclined his head. "Certainly not like the little girl I started tutoring two years ago."

I blushed. Usually he treated me as if I were still thirteen. But I preferred that to the way he was looking at me now. Had I known I would elicit such a look from him, I'd have worn sackcloth instead of my blue English gown.

"Jem, I've been telling John some of my adventures traveling through the county."

"Should you? Mr. Reid is a Tory."

"Jemima! John is our friend! And I think that's uncalled for. You should apologize."

"Mr. Reid doesn't apologize for being a Tory, do you, Mr. Reid?" I looked up at him.

"One should never apologize for one's beliefs, Jemima."

"Are you saying that if one believes in something or in doing something, they should do it?"

"Absolutely."

"Then why did you tell Father about David's activities this afternoon?" I asked.

"Jemima," Dan interrupted, "David is a child and he ran away from his responsibilities with Mr. Singer. As for John Reid's politics, they're his business. Our parents have opened our home to him. You know how it is in Trenton these days. Lots of Father's friends are Tories. Reverend Panton, for instance."

"He's different."

"Why?"

"Reverend Panton didn't go up to Boston last summer and mingle with the Tories and stay until autumn."

"Jemima! I'm ashamed of you! John Reid accompanied Mother and me to Becky's wedding. We couldn't have done without him in getting around a town held by the British."

"Then why didn't he come home with you and Mother after the wedding? Why did he stay on so long in a town held by the British?"

Dan set his mug on the mantel and turned to me. I could see why he would make a good officer. His scowl was fierce enough. "Jemima, I must insist that you apologize to John as a friend of this family and a guest under our roof."

There was nothing in his look to indicate that he would stand for anything less. But John Reid put a hand on his arm. "It's all right, Dan."

"It isn't," Dan insisted.

"Jemima is only provoking me, much the same as she does when I tutor her."

"And do you take this from her then? Constantly?"

John smiled. "I have my ways of getting back. Jemima will be doing extra doses of French and penmanship Friday, I can assure you."

Dan shook his head. "I don't know why you two can't get along. It makes me sad. I love you both. Jemima, it was your choice to have John for a tutor, wasn't it?"

"Only because if I didn't, I'd have to go to Miss Rodger's like Rebeckah, and learn to play the harpsichord and mingle with all those silly girls."

"Ah, you see John? You're the lesser of two evils."

Reid gave a mock bow. "Your sister's honesty is refreshing, and more than I enjoyed with Rebeckah, who wrote from Boston within two weeks of marrying a British officer that she loved me."

"Ah, Rebeckah." Dan reached for his coat and put it on. "My darling sister hasn't set foot in this house since she returned from Boston. You're well out of it with Rebeckah, John. Don't remind me of her. It's bad enough I have to go to Grandfather Henshaw's tomorrow and see her. Father's orders. No doubt Grandfather wants to talk to me about joining up. I was hoping you'd come along, Jem. You always can sweeten Grandfather's mood."

"Oh, can I come, Dan?"

He smiled. "If you apologize to John. The war is out there, and we'll all be involved in it soon enough. Let's not allow it to enter our lives just yet. I'd like you two to become friends before I go away."

He had me cornered. Reid saw it and took pleasure in it. "I'm sorry, Mr. Reid," I said. The haughty gleam in his eyes brought tears to my own as I ran from the room.

# CHAPTER

## 4

I lay in my bed under my warm quilt but I could not sleep. The December wind howled around the house, echoing my own mournful thoughts. The clock in the upstairs hall had chimed the half hour. Nine-thirty. I had heard Mother and Father come to bed at nine and David a few minutes earlier. Downstairs, Cornelius and Lucy, our house slaves, would now be retired in the small room off the kitchen where they slept.

From the parlor, underneath my room, I heard the voices of Dan and John Reid by the fire. I hadn't had the chance to tell Dan about Raymond Moore, who was probably at that moment making his way into our barn. Why did Dan spend so much time with a Tory?

All of the eligible men in Trenton were joining up, either with the American or the British army. All the Patriot women were using their spinning wheels to produce cloth for the army. Every Patriot family we knew had given up British goods and drinking tea. In St. Michael's, our church, half the congregation didn't speak to the other half because of the war, and there sat Dan, as friendly as ever with a Tory.

I put on my moccasins and wrapped myself in the heavy blanket that Grandfather Emerson, my father's father, had brought me from Hudson Bay.

The candles were burned down in the parlor, and in the semidarkness I saw Dan and Reid before the fire. I stood, half hidden, in the shadows of the hallway. "Dan."

He excused himself. "Jem, for heaven's sake, why are you up and about on a night like this?"

"I must talk to you."

"If it's about tomorrow, you know I said you could come along."

"Not about tomorrow."

"What then?"

I moved farther back into the hall, lowered my voice. "Dan, it will soon be ten o'clock."

"And did you come downstairs to tell me that?"

"No. I came to tell you that someone is waiting in the barn to see you. He wants to enlist."

In the candlelight he searched my face. "What are you telling me? Anyone who wants to see me can come to the house."

"If I tell you his name, you'll know why he doesn't dare."

"Then will you tell me? Or do we stand here playing games?"

"It's Raymond Moore."

"Moore? A Quaker? Are you daft, Jem? The Moores would never allow—"

"That's why he's in the barn, Dan."

He stood in silence as the enormity of what I'd said embraced him. "Raymond Moore! I'd never have guessed. He never said a word to me!"

"He came to me today in the street and begged me to

get word to you. He says he's been praying on his decision for weeks. His mind is made up, he says."

"Well, I'm glad *his* mind is made up. But where does that put me? His parents will never forgive me, and I'm about to ask for Betsy's hand."

"He says if you won't take him, he'll enlist elsewhere. And that Betsy won't blame you. If his mind is made up, mightn't his parents feel better about it if he served with you?"

"You certainly can make things sound simple."

"Raymond says it isn't seemly that others should fight for his land. Things are simple to him."

He sighed. "A good man. I'm honored he wants to sign on with me."

"You still need men. You said so yourself."

"I've seventy privates. I need six more. Since October when the Provincial Congress authorized a second battalion from this colony, it seems like half the county has knocked on our door in the middle of the night. But this is the first time I've had a recruit hiding in our barn like a runaway slave."

"Will you take him, Dan?"

"I'll talk with him first. Now go to bed."

"Dan, there's one more thing. Do you think Mr. Reid will tell about the musket?"

Over the rim of my candlelight he scowled at me. "He gave his word that he wouldn't. That's good enough for me. It should be good enough for you."

"I don't trust him, Dan. He's a Tory. How did he know Fitch was making gunlocks at the mill?"

"It's common knowledge in town. The Methodist Society is threatening to dismiss Fitch because he was doing it on the Sabbath. John is our friend, Jem. He would do nothing to hurt any of us. And you're only making it worse for yourself by provoking him."

"Is everything all right, Dan?" John Reid came toward us. It was not so dark that I couldn't see the amusement in his eyes at the sight of me in my flannel nightdress and blanket.

"If you two are plotting the overthrow of George the Third, you should at least do it by the warm fire."

"Jem was just going to bed," Dan said firmly.

"And I was just leaving." John put on his cloak. "Good night again, Jemima," he said, bowing. Dan walked him to the door. "I expect you to be your usual saucy self for your lessons on Friday," he said as he went out.

# CHAPTER
## 5

John Reid's words about Dan and me plotting to overthrow George the Third danced around in my head as I lay in bed. Sleep would not come. I lay watching the light snowflakes swirling against my window and seeing Reid's brown eyes filled with mockery. And lying there in the dark, it came to me. Ever since he had come home from Boston in September, Reid's mockery had boasted an air of assurance, as if he were privy to special information. There was nothing about him at all to indicate the rejected lover. It was too bad he hadn't married Becky. They deserved each other.

"Jemima, are you asleep?"

Mother stood in the doorway, a candle in one hand, a bundle in the other. "No, Mama, I haven't been able to."

"I heard you moving about. I've been lying awake myself, so I wanted to give you this to take to your sister tomorrow."

"Are you sending Becky a present after the way she's treated you?"

"Jem, Becky is still my daughter, no matter what she's done."

Had I done half of what Becky had done, I would have

been soundly punished for it. Of course, Grandfather Henshaw was a Tory, which was probably why she preferred to live with him. There he was, Mother's own father, and he and Mother barely spoke. They'd been at odds for months before fighting broke out up at Lexington, last spring. Right before that Becky had gone to Boston to visit Mother's sister, Aunt Grace. Another Tory. And when the fighting started in April, Becky just stayed on.

It was Aunt Grace who introduced her to the British officer, Lieutenant Oliver Blakely. And within weeks of meeting him, Becky was writing home saying she would marry. As if he were going to melt away on her in the summer heat.

David and I were recovering from measles, so we couldn't go. Dan and John Reid accompanied Mother, who said, seige or no seige, she wasn't going to be kept from her daughter's wedding.

The British held Boston, the harbor, and a few islands. The Americans settled in across the Charles River. And neither side could get to the other. Dan told me that only spies and travelers could get through.

Boston had been awful, Mother told us when she came back. The drought, the drain on provisions, and the heat had been intolerable. And there was fear of sickness, dysentery, and distemper. She worried about Becky for months. Then in November Becky came home to Trenton, leaving her husband in Boston, and went to live with Grandfather Henshaw.

Mother set down her candle and bundle and came to smooth my quilt. "It's only homespun for a cloak, Jem."

"Silk is more to Becky's taste."

"Well, silk has gone the way of our tea. Some of the finest women in Trenton are wearing homespun these days."

"Patriot women. And that leaves Becky out."

"Jem, I want no politics spoken between members of this family if it sets them apart."

I was about to say that Becky and I were already set apart and it hadn't taken a war to do it, but mother continued. "I want your promise that you'll act kindly toward Becky tomorrow."

"Mama, you know we never got along."

"I know you never tried. That's what I know."

"*She* was the one who provoked me when I shared this room with her. She chided me constantly."

"She was trying to teach you to be a lady."

"Well, if it means courting one man and marrying another right under his nose, I want no part of it."

Mama smiled. "I didn't know you had such sympathy for John Reid."

"I hate John Reid."

"You hate too easily, Jemima. John is an excellent tutor and he's fond of you."

"And that's why he brings his birch rod with him and sets it behind the door in Papa's study, I suppose."

"I have it on good authority that he's never used it in his school yet. The sight of it alone makes the boys behave."

"And so why does he bring it to our house?"

"He comes here directly from school. He brings all his things."

"And he isn't above setting it down with a flourish."

Mother's round face was serene, as always. "Jem, there is no more decent and gentle a man than John Reid. If your father and I weren't sure of that, he wouldn't be your tutor."

"Mama, how can you *say* that? He's a Tory! He's sneaky and mean. He told father about David being at the mill this afternoon, and he's mean to me when he teaches."

"Could it be that he's mean, as you say, Jem, because he can't control you? You ran off on him this afternoon."

I looked down at my quilt. "Did he tell you that, Mama?"

"It's true, isn't it?"

"Well, yes, but that's not the whole story. I meant to be back at lessons. I just lost my sense of time."

"He might be trying to teach you a sense of time, Jem. And responsibility. As well as sums and French. Did that ever occur to you?"

I was silent for a moment. "Mama, I only know that I don't like being tutored by a Tory. And when I went with Father last week to see the militia drill, Father said this quarrel we have with the king isn't likely to be made up without bloodshed. And John Reid's on the side of the king."

"Jem, do you remember last week when you told me you would never marry because, under this law of ours, once a woman marries she ceases to exist as a person? Do you remember that?"

"Yes."

"Do you remember what else you said?"

"I said I'd like to exist as a person for a while if it was all right with everybody."

"And when I told you that I never felt I'd ceased to exist as a person, married to your father, did you believe me?"

"Oh yes, Mama. You're more of a person than anybody I know!"

"Then believe me about this." She got up. "Believe me when I say that John Reid is a good man. People are much more than they appear on the outside. Why, when I was in Boston I even started to like Oliver Blakely. I found him to be very pleasant and considerate."

She kissed me and left. Sometimes I just didn't understand Mother. It was she who organized the Patriot women in town to boycott imported textiles and make their own liberty teas with sassafras or sage or strawberry. On one occasion she got the women to bring their spinning wheels to the courthouse yard where they worked spools of flax for a full day.

But talk of war or say something against someone she cherished, even if that person was a Tory, and she acted as if it had nothing to do with the war at all.

# CHAPTER
## 6

"Your mama say you're to be up right quick. Your mama say she never see such a lazy girl in the morning. Dan'l be out of the house on business two hours already."

I opened my eyes to see the sun streaming through my window and Lucy standing over me. "Your mama say breakfast be ready soon and your father be in from the shop any minute. And you know he don't tolerate no latecomers at the table. You be hearin' me?"

"I hear you, Lucy."

"Then sit up so's I know you're awake. Your mama say I'm not to come down and leave you to go back to sleep."

Lucy and her husband, Cornelius, were slaves, although you'd never know it the way they bossed us children around. A lot of families in Trenton had slaves. Even the Moores. But Mother was teaching ours to read and write. And Father was apprenticing Cornelius to Benjamin Smith to learn harnessmaking. They intended to set Cornelius and Lucy free one day.

It cost two hundred pounds to set a slave free, and they must be guaranteed an income of twenty pounds a year in earnings. But Father was determined to do it. My parents had endless discussions about it.

"You sleepin'?"

"No, Lucy, I'm saying my prayers."

"You bein' blasphemous, is what you doin'. And I aim to tell your mama if'n you don't get yourself out of bed this minute."

I sighed and pushed back the quilt and sat up. She stood, slim and erect and elegant in her homespun clothes. "I'm going to tell Mother you're slipping back into your careless ways of speaking if you tell her I was being blasphemous, Lucy."

"Put your feet on the floor and git up."

"The floor is cold."

She poured some water into the china washing basin, put another log on the fire, and handed me a piece of flannel. "Start washin'."

"You can read almost all of *Poor Richard's Almanac*, Lucy. And verses in the Bible that even I have trouble with. Mama works so hard with you. You can speak properly and you should at all times."

"John Reid...he works hard with *you*, too," she said.

"What does that mean?"

"You don't 'preciate what he does for you. You ran off yesterday when you was supposed to be learnin'."

"And so what if I did, Lucy?"

"So you're nobody to be tellin' Lucy what she should do. There's scented soap from your father's shop. Use it."

"Why do I get scented soap today?"

"Special. So you can smell sweet for your sister."

"I don't care a shilling's worth about smelling sweet for her."

"There's a new blue ribbon there, too. Your mama say

you're to wear it with your new printed English gown."

"I told you, Lucy, I don't care about your fine Miss Rebeckah."

"She ain't no miss no more. And she never was mine, anyway."

"She always was. You liked her manners. And you don't like me because I'm not prim and proper like her."

"I said start washin'."

"If I were Father, I'd never set you free, Lucy, do you know that? Never!"

She glided toward the door. "Hurry up," she said, "before the water gits cold."

Everything worth talking about in our family was discussed at mealtime. Breakfast was particularly noteworthy for this. When I got down to the kitchen the family was already assembled and eating.

We ate breakfast in the kitchen at the long oaken table. Cornelius had recently put a fresh coat of whitewash on the walls, and the usual assortment of dried herbs hung from the beams. The windows were without curtains, letting in plenty of light. The big cupboard in the corner held all of Mother's Delft plates, pewter, porcelain, and wooden bowls. The eight-foot fireplace was trimmed with blue and white tiles Father had imported from Holland, and there hung the oversized teakettle and brass and copper chafing dishes and all the other equipment Mother and Lucy needed for the constant cooking. It was a very friendly kitchen. But the look Father cast me as I slid into my place at the table was decidedly unfriendly.

"How long have you lived in this house, Jemima Emerson?"

"It will soon be sixteen years."

"And have you noticed, over those sixteen years, that breakfast in this house has always been at eight?"

"Yes, Father, I've noticed."

"Is this morning an exception?"

"I was dressing for my trip today. It took extra time."

He sipped his hot coffee and put a generous share of butter on his bread. My father's face, with his wisps of hair tucked behind his ears and his spectacles and finely chisled features, was the very image of a mild and loving parent. But he could manage sternness very nicely when the occasion warranted it.

For some reason he seemed to think it was warranted now.

"Jemima Emerson, I want a good account of your behavior today when you visit Grandfather Henshaw and Rebeckah. There is to be no talk of politics and no blame put at your sister's feet for her past actions. Is that understood?"

"I think so, Father."

"And you're to ride over in the chaise with Dan. You'll leave your horse in the barn today and give the creature a rest and act like a lady."

"But what do I do if Grandfather talks politics, Father? He's forever receiving news from Aunt Grace about Boston."

"You will politely change the subject, Jem," Mother said.

"But wouldn't that be rude?"

My father was glaring at me across the table. "Jemima, you aren't very high in my esteem for running off on your lessons yesterday, so I'd keep quiet for the rest of this meal if I were you. And don't talk with your mouth full in the first place."

"Yes, Father."

We continued eating. "Sarah, there are whispers in the merchant community that Thomas Riche is selling to the British army."

"And who is whispering such things, James? I tell you I don't believe it!"

The Riches were Philadelphia friends, dear to my parents. "We Patriot merchants have no proof," Father went on, "and I have seen his cash book. No wheat, flour, or pork is going to the British. He's been my friend for years, and I'll continue to send him goods from Trenton until I'm convinced I should do otherwise."

"John Fitch says most of the Philadelphia merchants are selling to the British." David saw his mistake as soon as he spoke the words, for now my father's steadfast gaze was upon him.

"He does, does he? Is that the kind of prattle he fills your mind with when you're at the mill with him?"

David said nothing.

"Do you know he's about to be expelled from the Methodist Society for repairing firearms on the Sabbath?"

"He's gunsmith for the Committee of Safety," David said. "It's his job."

"I'm quite aware that he's our gunsmith. Is it your job?"

"No, sir."

"John Fitch can do as he pleases. He's a good man and I've nothing against him. But when he drags you off from your responsibilities..."

"Nobody dragged me off. I went willingly."

"Then the fault is yours. Is that what you're saying?"

Again David saw his mistake. "I suppose you could say that."

"Then suppose you just cut an hour's worth of wood when you come home from Singer's this afternoon."

David mumbled something.

"What was that?"

"I said I don't see why I have to keep apprenticing to be a merchant when I'll be in the militia soon anyway."

"You'll be in the militia when I say you're ready, and not before."

Father was full of pepper in the morning. He put in an hour at the shop before breakfast and had plenty of time to formulate his early-morning discourses. Mother had told us to mollify him and not argue, that his bark was worse than his bite. But David was set to argue.

"You always said, Father, that betraying a confidence is just about the worst sin a man can commit, didn't you?"

Father reached for the pot of Mother's homemade raspberry jam. "If we're discussing sins, David, the field is wide open for comment. You'll be knee-deep in it if you're not careful."

"Didn't you?" David insisted.

"I did." Father always let us have our say. He dearly loved such discussions.

"Well, John Reid betrayed my confidence when he told you I ran off with Fitch yesterday."

"David!" Mother chided.

"It's all right, Sarah." Father waved off her dismay. "Did you confide in John that you were running off, then?"

"No, sir."

"Then there was no confidence to break."

Breakfast was over. Father pushed back his chair. "Sarah, you look tired." She had gotten up to hand him his blanket-coat.

"I was writing letters late last night, James."

"Does your sister Grace deserve such dedication?"

"I enjoy my letter writing."

He turned his attention to Dan. "Have you asked for Betsy Moore's hand yet?"

"I was going to do that today, Father."

"Well, do it, then. And stop dallying with that girl's feelings."

"It isn't my intention to dally."

"You're twenty, Dan. I was married to your mother at eighteen. At eighteen you court. At twenty, with war coming, you dally. Either do it today or have an end to it with her. And give the Moores our best when you stop by."

# CHAPTER
# 7

Grandfather Henshaw cried when he saw us. I had never seen a grown man cry, and I was unprepared for it. As for Dan, I think it unsettled him too because he just stood there on the front portico of the house with his tricorn hat under his arm while the old man shed his tears.

"Children, children," said Grandfather, opening his arms and crushing me against the velvet of his coat. "Come into the library, children, come, come." He dabbed his eyes with a silk handkerchief.

The library ran the whole length of the house. It had windows that looked out on lawns sloping to the Delaware River. The walls were lined with books, and a globe of the world and a telescope stood in front of the windows. He spent hours every day watching the barges go down the river to Philadelphia.

Grandfather Henshaw was a lawyer with a fine office in town. Dan planned to read law for his exams when his classical education at Princeton was finished, and so the two of them used to share much talk and intellectual argument. But the war came and Dan chose his side and joined up.

This was the first time he had seen Grandfather since doing so. But the old man said nothing as he led us in front of the crackling fire. A table was laid for lunch.

He poured wine for himself and Dan. I was given hot cider. The warmth and richness of the room made me sleepy after the long, cold ride. I sank down on the yellow damask sofa. A winter sun shone through yellow satin draperies, making the floors gleam where they weren't covered with carpets imported from Turkey. I never asked my mother, but I think her father was a very rich man.

"So, Daniel, you've done it. You've thrown your lot in with the Rebels."

"I prefer to call them Patriots, Grandfather."

"If it helps, call yourselves such. But it won't aid your cause. It makes me sad to see you go against your king."

"I have no king, Grandfather. The time for kings is past."

"Is the time for common sense also past?"

"I had hoped we wouldn't argue, Grandfather. It won't get us anywhere."

"You're right, dear boy, of course. It makes me even sadder, though, to see you give up your studies."

"I've all but finished my classical education. When the war is over there will be time enough to read law. Many of us are giving up a lot that we cherish these days. But we cherish our right to self-government even more."

"A fine sentiment, Daniel, and well spoken. But now let's eat, shall we?" He pulled a bell cord. A black man dressed in scarlet breeches came into the room accompanied by a black woman in gray with a white apron. Silently they laid out platters of cold turkey and beef, hot biscuits and honey, bowls of hot soup and preserved fruits. We sat at a round table near the fire. "Your sister will be down presently," Grandfather said.

"Let the children start. They must be famished."

How like Rebeckah to start out the visit by calling us children. She came into the room, beautifully gowned in dark green damask with ruffles. Dan and Grandfather rose, and you could see her astonishment as Dan towered over her.

"My, you look handsome. I can't believe how you've sprouted up. My little brother." She offered her cheek for a kiss.

There was less than two years' difference in their ages. She brushed her face against mine. "How are you, Jemima. Still as feisty as ever?"

We ate. Grandfather did most of the talking. He spoke of his farm and the weather and his law practice, which he was moving to Philadelphia, the center of cultural activity. And how he intended to pay a visit to our house before he left.

Rebeckah didn't bother with such niceties. "You didn't ride Bleu over, did you, Jem?"

"No, we came in the chaise."

"Heavens, you look as if you rode five miles on a horse."

"It's windy out there, Becky," Dan said firmly.

"So it is. How are your lessons, Jem? More to the point, how is John Reid? Does he ask after me?"

"He never mentions you, Becky," Dan said.

"Well, it was too brief a courtship to be worth mentioning. It didn't take me long to realize I didn't want to be married to a schoolmaster."

"I'd say it would be an improvement over a British officer," Dan said. He said it quietly so that Grandfather, who had taken his wine to the window, wouldn't hear.

Rebeckah laughed. "Our verbal dueling is one of the things I miss, not being home, Dan."

"I would have thought you'd miss other things."

She looked at him, her gray eyes troubled, and I could see that she realized she was no match for him anymore. "How is everyone at home?"

"Everyone is fine, Becky. I'll tell them you inquired."

"Yes, do. I should congratulate you on your commission, I suppose. Grandfather says you've raised your own company. You do look dashing. What militia group wears such a coat?"

"The Second New Jersey. We're not militia. We're Continental Line."

"I should hope not. The poor beggars didn't even have proper uniforms outside Boston. They were a rabble at Cambridge, I understand, when your Washington came to assume command in June. You couldn't tell them from the farmers."

"Probably because many of them were farmers. Proper uniforms or not, those poor beggars held their own at Lexington and Concord. Not to mention the way that rabble of an army has the British penned in Boston."

She got up. "Please don't talk of Boston. I left my husband there with General Howe, and I don't know if I'll see him again."

At this point Grandfather turned from the window. "Children, the river is so beautiful. Come look at it."

We went to stand beside him. "It's a moving, breathing, living thing," he said reverently. "It gives life to our town. It is deep in secrets and rich in dreams, and if we could know those secrets and dreams, we'd be a wiser people."

Grandfather always could turn a phrase, Mother said. The Delaware *was* beautiful, but frankly, I think he feared an argument was developing between Dan and Becky and wanted to distract them.

"Now," he said, "you brought a package for Becky, didn't you, Jem? Why don't you two go into the music room and have a nice visit. Dan and I have some business to talk over."

Becky soon made it clear to me that she had no intention of having a nice visit. She took the package, then said she had to oversee the help in the kitchen, as they were expecting guests for supper. As she left, she stopped in the doorway.

"Aunt Grace wonders why she receives so few letters from Mother. You may tell Mother she inquires after her."

"Mother writes to Aunt Grace all the time."

"Does she? How odd. Well, perhaps with the siege and all it's difficult for the mail to get through. Although I receive Aunt Grace's letters with little delay. Tell me, is John Reid really worming his way into Mother and Father's affections, as I hear from some friends in town?"

"If you want to know what's going on at home, Becky, you ought to visit and find out for yourself."

"Just as impudent as you ever were, Jemima, I can see that," she said, closing the door and leaving me to my own devices. I wandered around the room a bit. The large house seemed strangely silent. After a few minutes, though, I heard Grandfather's voice. It seemed to be getting louder and louder. Certainly he must be doing more than discussing business with Dan, since I could hear him clear across the wide hall.

I opened the door of the music room cautiously. The hall was deserted. I crept out and edged toward the closed library door.

"This is an intolerable situation, Daniel. Your mother's foolishness is going to get you all into trouble."

"Mother isn't a foolish woman, Grandfather."

"Nonsense. All women are foolish. It's in their nature. How can you take this so lightly? I don't think you realize what I said. Your mother is writing letters to the *Pennsylvania Gazette*, in support of the American army. Those letters are being published under the name of Intrepid. Letters, did I say? Why, they're a series of essays, I've been told. All calling for contributions of money and supplies. They've become so popular that other Patriot papers are reprinting them!"

"Mother always did write a fine hand, Grandfather."

"This is no time for impudence, Daniel. Let's be sensible. Our politics are different. As a well-to-do citizen I have much to lose with this social upheaval. Most men of influence are siding with the Crown. That your father chooses not to is his business. And I respect it. As I respect your right to fight for what you believe in."

"Thank you, Grandfather."

"However, not siding with the Crown and making activist moves against it are two different things. Your father has built a fine life for his family here in Trenton. If those letters came to light with the right authorities, he could lose everything he has."

"I don't think Father knows about the letters, if what you say about Mother is true, Grandfather."

"I'm sure he doesn't! Those letters are open acts of treason. Nothing less!"

I stood trembling out in the hall, shaken to the bone. I was trembling for Mama. The tone in Grandfather's voice was so urgent.

"My wearing this uniform is treason," Dan said.

"But you fight with your brother officers, under the command of an experienced general. Your Washington had years of experience in the French and Indian Wars. Your mother fights alone. Her pen is her only weapon. And if retaliation comes, she won't have an army with her. Be sensible, Dan. That's all I ask you to do."

"Exactly what are you asking me to do, Grandfather?"

"I called you here today to ask you to speak to your mother about the full consequences of her actions. Let her spin her cloth, if she will. Let her make her liberty teas. Such occupations are relatively harmless. I can't speak to your father. It would do no good. He wouldn't stop her anyway. Will you, for heaven's sake, speak to your mother? Will you do that?"

"I'll tell Mother of your concern, yes."

"Good. That's all I ask. She listens to you and respects your opinion. Now the day is turning cold. You should get your sister home. God be with you, Daniel. I hope to see you again before you go away."

# CHAPTER

## 8

Dan said not a word when we were back in the chaise and headed in the direction of the Moores'. I wrapped my cloak around me and huddled in an extra blanket. All I could think of was the conversation I'd overheard.

Mama was doing something that was treason! It wasn't liberty teas and spinning anymore. It was letters in support of our army! Letters good enough to be reprinted in other papers! A thrill went through me. How courageous of Mama! And all this while we thought she was spending those hours in her room writing to dotty old Aunt Grace. No wonder Aunt Grace wasn't receiving any letters.

"Dan?"

"What?"

"I want to tell you something."

"Go ahead."

"I hope you won't get angry."

"I do too. I've had enough to try me today."

"Dan, I heard what Grandfather told you. When you two were alone in the library. About Mama and the letters."

"How did you hear?"

"I was listening. I just happened to be in the hall and—"

"You eavesdropped?"

"Well, heavens, how could I help it? He was all but shouting."

"You could help it. You listened when you weren't supposed to. Damn, Jem, I'm beginning to think John Reid is right in some of the things he says about you. You had no *right* to listen!"

"Don't scold, Dan."

"I'll scold all I want to. It's a rotten habit, listening to other people's conversations. You've got some rotten habits, Jem."

"Dan, is it true that what Mother is doing is treason?"

"I refuse to discuss it with you."

"Please tell me. I don't want Mother to be hanged." I started to cry. And it wasn't difficult, concerned about Mother as I was and with the cold wind in my face.

"Now, stop that sniffling. Mother isn't going to be hanged."

"How do you know?"

"They don't hang women."

"What do they do to them?"

"How do I know what they do to them? She won't be caught anyway. Grandfather is just trying to frighten me into making her stop."

"Will you, Dan? Will you talk to her and make her stop?"

"I'll tell her the old man knows. She'll have to change her pseudonym."

"What's a pseudonym?"

"It's a name you write under to conceal your own. She'll have to find another so Grandfather thinks she's stopped. You know very well that nobody can talk Mother out of anything once she sets her mind to it. I don't know as I want to talk her out of it anyway."

"She's very brave, isn't she, Dan?"

"Damned if I know. I don't know what brave is. I've yet to find out."

"Is she foolish?"

"No. A person has to take a stand sometime if they're any kind of a person. She's doing a lot of good for our cause. We need the money and arms and clothing. We're poor, Jem, poor as church mice, our army."

"Will you tell Father?"

"No. The less he knows the better. He has enough on his mind. And you're not to either, you hear? If I find out that you told him, or anybody, I'll shake you until your teeth fall out. And I mean it."

He looked at me so fiercely that I shriveled up inside. "Promise me that you won't tell anyone."

"I promise."

"Good. Now straighten yourself up. The Moore farm is just down the road."


"Well, so thee's come to claim my Betsy, has thee?"

Mrs. Moore stood in the doorway of the white frame house, hands on her hips. Dan stood in front of her, holding his hat. "I would hope so, Mrs. Moore."

"How many times have I told thee to call me Ruth?"

"Ruth."

"Look me in the eye, Daniel Emerson. If thee can fight the British, thee can look me in the eye."

Dan looked her in the eye.

"Has thee been recruiting my Raymond?"

This was the awful moment Dan had been dreading. But he stood straight before her without guilt. "No, Ruth, I haven't recruited either of your boys. Raymond came and offered his services to me."

"And thee signed him on."

"Yes, I did."

"Why?"

"It was what he wanted. He feels he wants to fight for his land. I felt he was of age and had put a good deal of thought into his decision."

"Thee puts it plain enough." She sighed. "My boys have been to town several times to watch the militia drill and to exchange ideas. Isaac and I know Joseph will soon follow his brother. I'll not hold thee responsible for Raymond's decision."

"I'll feel responsible for him just the same, Ruth."

She nodded. "Look at thee, Daniel Emerson. I see thee and I know that if thy convictions fit as well as thy coat, I'll have no quarrel with thee."

"I'm comfortable with my convictions. I think Raymond is, too."

She embraced him, then me. "Isaac is in the barn. I know thee wants to speak with him. Come into the house, Jemima. We can talk."

"Are thy parents well?"

"Yes, thank you, Ruth," I answered.

She was kneading dough in a large wooden bowl. Over the fire a chicken was on the spit. Betsy Moore sat at the wooden table cleaning vegetables. I liked Betsy, but we had never been what you would call friends. Now she would most likely be betrothed to Daniel. I looked at her as if I'd never seen her before. She was very pretty, even in her plain Quaker clothes. She had beautiful skin, rich curly hair, a narrow waist, and a full bosom, and it was not difficult to see why Dan was attracted to her. More than that, though, she was sharp of mind and devoted to Dan.

"How are thy lessons?" Ruth asked.

"My lessons are fine."

"Betsy doesn't fare well in school. The girls taunt her because she's a Quaker."

"I'm sorry, Betsy." I looked at her. "I never did think much of the girls at Miss Rodger's anyway."

"I go for the music and the lessons," Betsy said, "not for the company. Thee is lucky to have a tutor, Jem."

"You wouldn't think so if you knew how he treats me. Being tutored by him is only one step better than going to Miss Rodger's."

"Thy mother says he thinks thee has much common sense and spirit," Ruth Moore said.

"You must be talking about somebody else, Ruth. John Reid accuses me, half the time, of being dim-witted. He's forever scolding, and I think he hates me."

"Thee can be blind sometimes." She smiled. "I think thy mother chose wisely in having thee tutored privately. I committed the sin of pride in sending Betsy to Miss Rodger's, and now she suffers. Added to the taunts is the fact that the other girls board there, so she has no friends."

"Mother, I don't want such friends," Betsy put in.

"Thee walks alone," Ruth accused her. "What thee will do when Dan leaves, I cannot think."

"I could spend some time with Betsy, Ruth," I offered.

"Thee is kind, Jem. She loves to walk in town and look in the shop windows. People think Quakers are priggish, but we like our fun."

I could have told her that Betsy wasn't priggish. I'd seen how she acted the few times I'd observed her with Dan, and if there was one word that I wouldn't use to describe her, it was *priggish*.

"Are thy parents still speaking of setting Lucy and Cornelius free?"

"Yes."

She kneaded her dough with even more fervor. "Sometimes I wonder what kind of people we are to speak of liberty and still keep slaves. It causes much controversy in Meeting. Isaac and I have decided to follow in thy parents' footsteps. It will be difficult setting our two slaves free with the boys joining up, but we will manage."

Mr. Moore and Dan stood in the doorway. Behind them the late-afternoon winter sky was heavy and threatening. A blast of cold air followed them into the kitchen. Their faces were ruddy from tramping the farm, and Mr. Moore's eyes were solemn. We all turned to look at him.

"Put up some coffee, Ruth. And set out the fresh carrot pie. These two young people have something to celebrate."

"Oh, Papa, thank you." Betsy ran to him, hugged him, then fell into Dan's embrace.

"For the most part we Quakers do not look kindly on our children marrying out," Mr. Moore said, hanging his flat-brimmed hat on a peg. "But we have been friends with thy family so long, Jemima, and we are honored." He took my face in his hands and kissed it. His hands were icy-cold. "Welcome into the family," he said.

# CHAPTER
# *9*

Nothing much happened in the next three weeks that would have warranted the struggle with my goose quill pen to record it. My penmanship was still abominable, anyway. Goodness knows, I tried, but I'd all but given up in my attempts to master the art. Had it not been for John Reid standing over me three days a week and browbeating me into practicing, much as he browbeat me to learn French and Latin, I would have quit the whole business and been done with it.

We did have a fine feast at Christmas. I worked for days helping Mother and Lucy prepare the winter pea soup, sweet potato biscuits, clam pie, corn bread, cider spice cake, and venison stew. Mother said our table would be the finest she had ever prepared. She didn't elaborate, but I knew she was thinking of the war and wondering if we'd all be together again next year.

The table was laid in our great hall, so called because it ran down the center of the house and was wide enough for dining or dancing. Rebeckah and Grandfather Henshaw finally condescended to come. The Moores were there too, as was Reverend Panton. But the best part of all was the presence of Grandfather Emerson, my father's father. He lived five miles outside town on his estate, Otter Hall. He was very tall and wiry, with a gentle grace about him that tall men often have. He had served with Washington and Braddock when they drove the French from their forts on the Ohio River twenty years before. He always wore frontier clothing because he'd spent years in French Canada, where he'd traded furs and pelts with the Indians.

He entertained us with stories about General Washington. And if that wasn't enough to make the day worth noting, Raymond Moore seated himself next to me at the table and we had the most pleasant conversation.

"I never can thank thee enough for helping me out when I wanted to join up, Jemima."

"Well, goodness, we're friends. It was the least I could do."

"Thee has so much more spirit than most girls I know. I hope thee won't forget me while I'm away."

"Forget you? How could I? I'm not a fickle girl who forgets someone she admires."

"Thee admires me, Jemima?"

"How could I not? I think I always have admired you, Raymond."

"I would be honored if thee said I could write to thee."

"Of course you can. I'll write to you too. I'd enjoy getting your letters and corresponding. And anyway, it's the least I can do when you're off fighting for liberty."

All the while John Reid was eyeing me sternly across the table. And when the time came for giving toasts, he stood up after Father and Dan and my two grandfathers had given theirs.

"To Sarah and James Emerson, two dear friends who

have been like parents to me. To all our dear friends here assembled, whose friendship outshines politics, and"—he turned to me—"to my little charge, Jemima, who is by far the best student of Latin I have ever had."

I blushed. I wanted to run from the table. Everyone's eyes were upon me, and I felt hot and cold and very much the fool—until I saw Rebeckah looking at me with pure hatred. Then I felt a surge of happiness, which confused me even more.

I cornered him in the parlor after our meal. "Mr. Reid, you know I do poorly in Latin. What ever made you say such a thing?"

"Ah, Jemima, you may do poorly, but you're still by far the best student of the language I've ever had. You're always accusing me of scolding. Can't you tolerate a little praise?"

"Not when I don't deserve it. I'd rather be scolded than flattered unjustly for your own reasons."

"And what may those reasons be?"

"You're still fond of Rebeckah. You said it to make her jealous."

His good nature vanished and his face darkened. "You're more of a child than I thought, to say such a thing. And if it's scolding you want, you'll get it. How can you promise to write to Raymond Moore when your penmanship is such a disgrace?"

"What business is it of yours if I write to him?"

"He won't understand your chicken scratching."

"Why, then, you'll just have to help me improve my penmanship, won't you?"

"Indeed, I will. Under the condition that no letter goes to Raymond until I approve it first to make sure it's legible."

"If you think, for one minute, that I'm going to allow you to read my correspondence—"

"That's the only way you'll be writing to him. I hope I'm to have some pride in my tutoring. As long as I approve your letters, you can write your little head off to him about how proud you are that he's away fighting for liberty."

"At least he'll be off fighting for what he believes in, which is more than I can say for some people!"

He was smiling when I flounced away, showing his beautiful white teeth. Men are so vain, I thought, forever showing off what nature may have blessed them with.

The militia was drilling once a week in Trenton by the time of the new year. Up north our army was still dug in across the Charles River from the British. One day I found David out behind the barn going through the whole manual of arms with Dan's musket. Most likely he thought that only Chauncy the goat was watching until he saw me. Then he begged me not to tell Father. I said I wouldn't, which gave me two secrets to keep.

I hadn't told anyone about Mother's letter writing. She was still staying up late by candlelight writing at least two nights a week. She had also organized her Ladies for the Promotion of Frugality and Industry to make shirts for the army. When I didn't have lessons I joined them twice a week.

Then one Sunday morning in January Father produced a copy of the *Pennsylvania Gazette* at breakfast and announced that he would read a letter by someone called Libertus. Under the table Dan kicked me. And I knew that Mother had found her new pen name.

Mother's face was very white. "James, this is the Lord's Day."

"My dear, the Lord Himself could have inspired this essay. It addresses the womenfolk, reminding them that their willingness to sacrifice should match the courage of the men in the field."

"The women in Trenton *are* sacrificing, James."

"I don't understand your resistance to hearing this."

"It isn't proper conversation for the Sabbath."

"As far as I know, that has never stopped us from discussing anything in this house." Father was about to say more when Dan stood up.

"I'd like to be excused, Father."

"Excused? From what? Breakfast? You not hungry? Impossible."

"Breakfast and services. I can't go to church and pray for the king."

"Ah." Father took off his spectacles, intrigued by the possibility of the discussion. "Nobody expects you to pray for the king."

"Reverend Panton always includes prayers for him in the services."

"So he does. And do you know why?"

"Because Reverend Panton is a Tory."

"Not so simple, Dan. As a condition of his ordination in the Church of England he has taken an oath of the king's supremacy. To depart from that oath would be to break his solemn vows."

"Well, I took no such vows. My loyalties are to our Cause."

"As they should be. But we still belong to the Church of England. So we go to services. But we don't have to join in the prayers for the king. Many remain silent."

"I know that. But I also know that the whole parish is torn. And that church is a hotbed of controversy. Why go and practice hypocrisy? You always said hypocrisy is the worst sin of mankind."

"Second only to rudeness, Dan. Civility is all we have

left in times of war. As an officer, you should know that."

"As an officer in the Continental army I know one thing, Father. That I have no place in a church where prayers are said for George the Third—or any king."

Silence followed. At least Dan had diverted Father from his essay reading. Father took a piece of pumpkin bread and spread it liberally with butter, regarding Dan. "Yes," he said quietly, "I can understand that. Where are you off to, then?"

"I have a meeting."

"A meeting? On the Sabbath?"

"We leave tomorrow. It can't be helped."

Father nodded. "Very well, Dan, if your mother agrees, I will excuse you."

Of course, Mother agreed. "I'm sure you will pray in your heart, won't you, Dan?"

"I'll be sure to do that, Mother." He kissed her on the way out. How I envied him, coming and going as he pleased. I pushed my food around on my dish.

"Eat your breakfast, Jemima," Father ordered. "And stop slouching at the table."

"I'm not hungry."

"If you think that by mimicking your brother you'll be excused from services, you're wrong. So you might as well eat."

"Would you excuse me from services?" David asked.

"Do you have problems saying prayers for the king?"

"I'm one of the people who doesn't say them. I keep quiet."

"Good. Put that into practice now and eat."

"John Fitch says St. Michael's will soon be closing. Too many vestrymen are Tories."

"How John Fitch knows so much about the Anglican

Church when he's a Methodist is beyond me."

"He knows a lot about what goes on in town," David insisted.

"So it seems. He could start his own newspaper. Trenton could use one. But until he does, I'd like to read mine."

"Father, I have to ask you something," I said.

He sighed. "Is there no peace for a man in his own home on the Sabbath? What is it, Jemima?"

"I've promised to write to Raymond Moore while he's away."

"Since you've already promised, I don't see the problem."

"John Reid insists on reading my letters first."

"And why is that?"

"He says my penmanship is a disgrace and as my tutor he can't allow a letter to go off unless he inspects it."

He smiled.

"Well, goodness, Father, I don't see what's so funny. Why should he be allowed to read my letters?"

"Jemima, first, your penmanship *is* a disgrace. And second, one of these days you will understand the humor of his purpose. And when you do, God willing, you'll be mature enough to not mind John inspecting your correspondence."

"Now whatever is that supposed to mean? Mama, please can't you help?"

"John means no harm dear. Do as he wishes."

"You always defend him! Both of you! He has more privileges in this house than any of us!"

"Jemima!" Father said sternly. "You will conduct yourself as a proper young lady of Christian upbringing in this house on the Sabbath or you will be confined to your chamber for the day. Now, which will it be?"

He knew which it would be. I calmed myself. The bells of St. Michael's were ringing. Well, at least Dan and I kept Father from reading the essay and upsetting Mama.

# CHAPTER
## *10*

In the west the sky was still dark, and the houses and shops loomed against it in unnatural shapes. But in the east the sun was streaking the sky with red.

Like blood, I thought. I shivered and pulled my blanket coat around me. All up and down our street Dan's men were assembling to go off to war on that cold January morning. Some brought their womenfolk with them.

The Moores were there. I saw Raymond in the distance, and he sighted me immediately and came over and took off his hat. He had a fine new musket, and with his cartridge box and canteen and powder horn, he looked like a soldier. Lanterns flickered in the morning cold and families huddled with their men for the last time. Horses and men alike breathed spurts of white breath. Dan and his officers were everywhere, checking off names and inspecting equipment. Some children whimpered in their mothers' arms, and a few dogs mingled with the crowd, wagging their tails at the excitement.

Lucy stood next to me holding a lantern and a small bundle. Cornelius held the reins of Dan's horse, Gulliver.

How many times I, on Bleu, and Dan, on Gulliver, had ridden over to the Moores'. Now Gulliver was going off to war. I couldn't bear thinking on it.

"I would speak with thee, Jemima." Raymond Moore took my arm and led me away from the lantern light. "Thee will look after Betsy while I am gone?" He peered down earnestly into my face, his eyes filled with unspoken longings.

"I'll look after her, Raymond. And oh, I'll miss you. And I am proud of you for . . . for going against everyone and joining up."

"Jemima . . ." He almost croaked my name. Then he looked about wildly to see who was watching, pulled me farther into the morning dark, took me by the shoulders, and kissed me.

I was too surprised to resist, and then, after I got through being surprised, I didn't want to resist anymore. The last thing in the world that I wanted to do was resist, as a matter of fact. It was very nice in his arms and I wished it would never end. But it did. He pulled back, confused and embarrassed.

"I hope I haven't offended thee."

"You could never offend me, Raymond."

"Jemima, remember thy promise to write."

He was moving away. I knew in my heart that I would never forget the way he stood looking at me in the middle of the confusion that day. "I'll write, Raymond."

Dan was shouting commands and the men, about fifty of them, fell into some sort of order. They would rendezvous with another twenty-five or so along the way to Princeton. I saw Dan go to Mother and Father and Betsy and say goodbye. Then he murmured some words to David, shook Cornelius's hand, and hugged Lucy, who gave him the bundle. He was in full dress, wearing epaulets on his shoulders, a sword and pistols, and a cocked hat. He looked very capable and dashing.

"Jemima." He was looking down at me.

I couldn't bear any more goodbyes. "Dan, I don't want you to go."

"None of us wants to go. But it's our duty. Will you look after Mother and Betsy?"

"Goodness, if one more person asks me to look after Betsy..."

"I saw you with Raymond." He smiled. "Is that what he was doing? Asking you to look after Betsy?"

I blushed. "Dan, could you really kill people?"

"I don't think about killing."

"But you will if you have to?"

"I'll do what I must. As you will. Don't worry about killing. War is mostly marching and encampments and drilling and boredom. Jem, listen to me. Grandfather Emerson knows about Mother and the letters."

"What?"

"He mentioned it to me. Mother confided in him. You know those two have always gotten along. It's all right. There's no better Patriot than he."

"I'm glad he knows."

"Yes. You can confide in him, if you must. But no one else. And don't mention it to Mother. Let her keep her secret. And one more thing. Be kind to John Reid."

"How can you think of him at a time like this?"

"Because he's a dear friend. More dear than you could know. And although you two are always fighting, he holds you in high esteem."

"I won't argue with you because you're leaving."

"Then don't. Trust me. Things are not always what they

seem with people. Goodbye for now, Jem. I'll write." He embraced me. His hold was fierce, his face cold, and, pulling away, he brushed my face with his hand. He walked to his horse, which Cornelius still held, mounted, gave an order, and then they were all moving down the street. They would pick up their two musicians in Penny Town, so there was no music now, just their steady rhythmic shuffling and the creak of their wagons as they marched off into the mist.

The houses hovered over us protectively. A cock crowed, a dog barked, and the lanterns added an eerie light to the awful, silent scene. I stood rooted as they marched past the red frame house of Sam Bellerjeau, Dr. Bellvidere's stable, Ethan Downing's house, and Benjamin Smith's, then past Third Street and Thomas Tindall's fine house of brick.

This wasn't the way it was supposed to be, I thought. It was all too desolate, too final. I had never thought that anything could be as empty and final as seeing them march off like that. I'd gone several times with Father to see our militia drill. It had always been under blue skies. The drums had been drumming to quicken the blood. And the fifes had been playing saucy tunes. There had been a gaiety and excitement about it.

There was no gaiety and excitement now. There ought to be more to it, I decided. All around me people were leaving, going back home. "Come along, Jem," Father said.

But I stood there until I felt a hand on my arm. "Come on in," Lucy said. "We be havin' fresh-baked bread and strawberry preserves for breakfast."

In the kitchen I sat numbly, shivering, still in my blanket-coat, while my family ate. Mother had gone upstairs. David and Father ate in silence and left to do their respective chores. Cornelius went about his work out in the barn.

"He be all right," Lucy said. "Dan'l is one smart boy."

"It's all wrong, Lucy. A person shouldn't go off to war like that. There ought to be more to it."

"What more is there?"

"I don't know. Drums. I think there should be drums."

"Drums on the battlefield. Time enough for drums. Eat now."

I ate. The morning light came through the windows. I never knew that a person's soul had such depths as I felt, sitting there. And I still thought there ought to be more.

# CHAPTER

## *11*

After breakfast I had chores, and since it was Monday, John Reid was coming in the afternoon. I couldn't bear the thought of lessons that day. I didn't know if anybody could undo my soul more than it was undone already. But I knew one thing—John Reid would try.

There was only one person in the world I wanted to see, and that was Grandfather Emerson. So I slipped out of the house and saddled Bleu and was off, cutting across our property to Second Street. At the corner I headed up King to DeCow's Alley and out to River Road. The morning wind whipped my hair and the ground blurred beneath Bleu's hooves. Once out on River Road, I let the tears come. They fell into Bleu's mane as he carried me along.

Grandfather Emerson had three hundred and fifty acres of farmland on River Road. All his help was hired, for he would not keep slaves. He lived with an Indian servant or an Indian friend—I wasn't quite sure what the young man known as Broken Canoe was to him.

I'd heard gossip that Canoe was his son by a second wife, an Indian woman he'd left up in Canada. I had never asked my father about it. Father was always friendly to Canoe, but Canoe never visited our house and hardly ever came to town. I never held with gossip. All I knew was that Grandfather's first wife had died when my father was a boy in 1745 and that Canoe was twenty-seven.

I figured that what Grandfather did with any woman in Canada after his wife died was his business. He still made trips to Canada every so often and traveled among the Indians. He had their respect and was invited to all their treaty-making assemblies.

He never scolded me for being unladylike. He had a white beard, and I knew that my father visited him often for quiet talks and counsel. I did too, but not as much as I would have liked.

About half a mile before the farm Bleu surged forward with a new burst of energy, his muscles straining. I held on, but while I was cutting across a field to Grandfather's barns, he tripped. I didn't have enough of a grip on the reins, and I flew right over his head and hit the ground hard, landing on one hand.

Everything was upside down for a moment, spinning. I sat on the frozen ground, stunned. There was a narrow brook nearby, and Bleu was drinking out of it with as much concern for me as John Reid had when I cried after one of his scoldings.

I jumped up and grabbed the reins. He shouldn't be drinking so greedily after such a workout. He was glistening with sweat, and Grandfather would scold me for allowing him to become overheated. I dipped my wrist into the water, and it was so cold tears came to my eyes. I started shivering. I was feeling poorly, as a matter of fact, so I began to walk slowly across the field in the direction of Grandfather's house. But by the time I was halfway across, the wrist was hurting to the point of distraction and I was almost faint with my efforts.

It was Canoe who saw me coming. He was near the stables and came running. I handed the reins wordlessly to him, but he scooped me up instead and carried me across the rest of the field. Bleu followed.

"Jemima Emerson, did that horse throw you?"

"No, Grandfather, it was my fault, truly."

"And how was it your fault?"

"I was riding too fast. I didn't hold his head up when he tripped."

"Your parents never did like the fact that I gave him to you. You'll break your neck one of these days and they'll disown me."

"I won't break my neck, Grandfather."

Canoe had carried me through the huge center hall where Grandfather's beloved hunting dogs had come to greet us. From the large rooms beyond, two Indian women on moccasined feet approached. Canoe set me down on the sofa. Relics of Grandfather's trips north were all around, and the wide floorboards were covered with woven Indian rugs.

One of the Indian women washed my face. The other attended to my wrist, and in no time at all it felt better.

Grandfather watched me all the while. "You're exactly like I am, Jemima Emerson," he said. "You like to run free and lead your own life and not account to anyone. A certain amount of that is fine, but we do have to conform to some rules in this world. Now tell me, why were you riding so fast?"

"I was anxious to see you."

He scowled. "You've been crying. Why?"

"Because I fell."

He thanked the Indian women and they left. "Now you

can tell me why you were crying." He looked at me steadily.

"Because everything's so awful."

"What's awful?"

"Dan left today. And Raymond Moore."

"Ah, the Moore boy. The Quaker who joined up. I met him Christmas Day. I saw you and him talking at the table. You're fond of him?"

"I suppose you could say that."

"And do you suppose he returns your esteem?"

"Yes."

"And so, breaking your neck is going to make you feel better?"

"Well, there's everything else, too."

"What else?" He stood, unyielding, while I recited my list of woes. In the background was Canoe, arms crossed on his chest, wearing the same frontier clothes as Grandfather. He was very striking and dignified and tall. He didn't smile, but his eyes were most sympathetic.

"So," Grandfather said, "you ran off on your family, you'll not be home for lessons, you've muddied and torn your clothing, sprained your wrist, and run your horse half to death. How do you expect me to make this day come out right for you, little lady, when you've done so much to make it wrong?"

"You always could, before." I started to cry.

He sat down next to me. "Jemima, I won't pretend your troubles aren't real. But you've brought many of them upon yourself today. I know you worry about Dan and your friend. But Dan was here last evening to say goodbye. He's capable and he has sense. He knows when to be brave and when not to be foolish. I promise you, he'll come through."

I hugged him. "I haven't told you everything yet."

"What else is there?"

But I couldn't say. He understood. He signaled Canoe with a nod of his head, and Canoe left.

"Your mother and her letter-writing campaign, is that it? Dan told me you knew. That's a lot for someone your age to keep her own good counsel about." He took my hands in his own. "Listen to me. I've just given a considerable amount of money to Washington for the army. I can tell you, it's needed. On Breed's Hill our army would have won outright if they hadn't run out of musket balls. Would you want that to happen to Dan someday?"

"No."

"The support your mother is raising could someday help Dan and the Moore boy and others. We're all going to be called upon to do our part before this thing is through. Be proud of your mother."

He wiped my tears, then called the Indian women to come back. One brought tea made with herbs, the other cornmeal pudding mixed with bits of meat and nuts and dried berries. There were cakes that I didn't recognize. We ate, and then Grandfather made me lie down and rest. He covered me with a blanket, and I was left alone to sleep. I awoke to find him kneeling over me with Canoe standing nearby. I was to start for home, he said, and Canoe would ride with me. I protested that I could ride alone, but he wouldn't hear of it.

"I have a visitor coming this afternoon, or I'd take you myself. Canoe will take my place. Anytime you need to talk, I'm here. You know that." He kissed me goodbye. Canoe took me to the kitchen, where I was given warm cider and I washed my face. Outside he lifted me onto Bleu, and we began the ride home.

We rode in silence for a while. From my past visits to Grandfather's farm I knew that Canoe would talk when he

was ready and that he wouldn't talk if he didn't like someone. After the first mile he started to tell me about his
boyhood in Canada, of how Indian children are never punished and are allowed to run free. At the outskirts of town
he dismounted and handed me a bag of pemmican, which
is made of dried buffalo meat mixed with fat and dried
cranberries. He gave me a bag every time I visited. I kept
it in a small chest in my room. Someday, if the British ever
came to Trenton, I would have it, for it was an emergency
ration. And then, whatever else happened, we wouldn't be
hungry.

# CHAPTER
## *12*

As I rode Bleu slowly up Queen Street I could see Grandfather Henshaw's carriage in front of our house. It was piled high with baggage. I felt sick with foreboding. Now I not only had Mother to face but Grandfather and Rebeckah as well. I brought Bleu to the barn and took my time feeding and watering him. Then I went into the house the back way and was about to slip up the stairs when Rebeckah called from the parlor.

"You might have the decency to come and say hello, Jemima."

They were having coffee. A cheery fire was burning on the hearth. Grandfather Henshaw was seated on one side of the fireplace, Mother on the other. John Reid was perched on a window seat. Rebeckah, in scarlet silk, stood in the middle of the room.

"Jem, what happened?" Mother jumped up when she saw me.

"I'm all right, Mama. I took a spill riding Bleu and hurt my hand, but the Indian women at Grandfather Emerson's bandaged it for me. It's much better now."

"Grandfather Emerson's! Is that where you were! And I've been sitting here worrying about you! Jemima, how can you be so inconsiderate?"

"I'm sorry, Mama." I was suddenly aware of my torn and muddy petticoat and disheveled appearance.

"You look a fine mess, I must say." Rebeckah stepped forward. "Did it ever occur to you that Mother may have wanted you here today, after Dan left? You never change, do you, Jem?"

For the life of me I could think of no reply. They were all looking at me accusingly. John Reid watched me knowingly, but said nothing.

"Honestly, Jemima, sometimes I don't know what to do with you anymore," Mama was saying. "I sent John out to look for you. He searched all over town. Why did you go to Grandfather Emerson's?"

"Because she was off on one of her wild jaunts again with no thought for anyone but herself, that's why," Rebeckah said. "She ought to be whipped for worrying you so."

"You're one to talk," I shot back. "You haven't had any consideration for Mother since you've been home!"

"How dare you?" She stepped forward and grasped my good arm. "You little ruffian, how dare you speak to me like that."

"I speak the truth. You've given Mother more heartache than anybody."

She drew back her arm to slap me, but the next thing I knew John Reid was there restraining her. "That's enough, Rebeckah. It isn't your place to punish her."

"Whose is it? Yours? You can't even keep her from running off on her lessons when Mother is paying you so dearly. She's out cavorting with Indians instead."

Reid laughed. "So your grandfather Emerson is an Indian, eh? I knew there was some reason I didn't marry you."

"Your grandfather Emerson is not an Indian, Rebeckah," Mama said, sharply.

"Well, he might as well be. He's married to one. If he is, indeed, married. No wonder Jem feels so at home there, with that Indian servant, or whatever he is to Grandfather, hanging around."

"You leave Canoe out of this," I said. "He's a good person. He escorted me to the outskirts of town."

"Thank *heaven* he had the sense to stay on the outskirts. At least everyone didn't see you riding with that savage."

"He's not a savage!"

"Dear, dear, this is intolerable." Grandfather Henshaw sat mopping his brow.

"Rebeckah! Jem! For heaven's sake, show some consideration for your mother, both of you!" John Reid spoke in his best schoolmaster's tone.

Rebeckah calmed herself. "It wouldn't be intolerable if Mother would take my suggestion," she said. "I tell you, Mother, you'd do the right thing if you let me take her to Philadelphia."

The room was suddenly silent. Mother had turned and was standing at the window, her back to us, rigid and silent.

"Mama? That isn't why Becky and Grandfather are here, is it? You're not sending me to Philadelphia." I saw the smug look on Becky's face and started to understand.

"You'd learn how to behave in civilized company at least," Becky said. "One year in Philadelphia with me and you'd learn manners. I can promise you that."

"Mama?" My voice cracked and my heart was hammering inside me.

"Go upstairs, Jem," she said without turning around, "and clean yourself up and rest."

The sobs started deep inside me and then the tears came. I didn't know where to look. I put my hands to my face.

"Come here, Jem." It was John Reid's voice, but I didn't move.

"Jemima Emerson, I said to come here." He used his schoolmaster's tone again. Numbly I went to him.

He looked at me, his brown eyes intent but not unkind. "Now, listen to me. Rebeckah says I can't do anything with you. Do you want to prove her right?"

I couldn't speak. I shook my head no.

"It looks as if I can't. Not only to Rebeckah, but to your mama right now. She would have every right to terminate my services today. It seems as if I've failed as your tutor. Perhaps the only thing left for your mother to do is send you to Philadelphia."

"I don't want to go to Philadelphia, Mr. Reid," I appealed.

"Then do as I say, and perhaps we can redeem this day. There will be no packing you off right now, not until your parents discuss this. So go to your sister and grandfather and kiss them goodbye."

"Kiss Rebeckah?"

"Yes."

"I won't."

"You will do as I say!" His eyes flashed and his voice held a dozen familiar threats. I went and kissed them.

"Dear child," Grandfather said, wiping his eyes. He was quite beside himself. "Mind your tutor, there's a good girl."

Rebeckah accepted my kiss coolly. "Grow up, Jem. You must, sooner or later, you know."

"Mama?" I looked at her, but she wouldn't turn around.

"Leave your mother be, Jem," Reid directed, "and come

along with me." He took hold of my good wrist and pulled me from the room. Closing the door, he looked at me. "You've all but ruined things for yourself today, you know that, don't you?"

I said nothing. I was nearly falling off my feet with exhaustion.

"Your sister's been working on your mother for two hours to take you to Philadelphia. If you think I'm bad, try having her for a teacher. You'd come crawling back in two months."

"Thank you, Mr. Reid."

"For what? I've done nothing yet. You're still in danger of going. Your mother is at her wit's end with you. If you'll take my advice, you'll go to your chamber until after supper and pretend exhaustion. Which shouldn't be too difficult, the way you look. At the table I'll try to smooth things over with your parents."

"Why would you do that for me?"

He smiled. "If you think I'm going to let Rebeckah have anything to do with the way you turn out after I've invested two years in you, you have another think coming. Besides, I owe more than that to your parents."

He kept his eyes down while he spoke. I moved toward the stairs.

"Jemima."

"Yes, Mr. Reid."

"I'll fight for you to stay. All I have to fight with is my promise to your parents that I can do a good job with you. If I win and they let you stay, things will be different with us, however. There will be no more nonsense. I won't tolerate it. Do we understand each other?"

I looked at him, thinking of how I hated him and here he was offering me the only hope I had at the moment. "Yes, Mr. Reid," I said. I ran up the stairs.

# CHAPTER
## 13

I awoke to a knock on my door. "Jem?" I roused myself and opened it to find David. "Jem, you're wanted downstairs."

"Who wants me?" I rubbed the sleep from my eyes. It was dark except for David's candle. "What time is it?"

"It's near eight. Supper's over. You should have been there. All they did was talk about you."

"What did they say?"

"I'm not supposed to tell you. But John Reid took your part. Whatever you did today, I hope you had fun, because you're to be punished for it. When I came home for my noon meal there was all hell to pay because everyone was looking for you. Mother thought you took Bleu and followed Dan to Princeton."

"Did they say anything about Philadelphia?"

"You're not going. Reid told Father at supper that he'd take full responsibility. He said he intended to make something of you. I wouldn't want him making something of me, Jem. Damned Tory. I think you would have been better off going to Philadelphia."

"David, stop your swearing. Where's Mama?"

"She's gone to bed. She's feeling poorly. I told them at supper that Dan had given me his musket when he left, and Mama cried and Father said if I mentioned that musket again, he'd hit me. I think everybody's gone daft. Jem, did you kiss Raymond Moore when he left this morning?"

"Who said anything about that?"

"Father knows about it. Someone saw you and told him. And I thought I was bad running off and making gunlocks with John Fitch. You'd better get downstairs, Jem, they're waiting. You'd better do something about the way you look, too."

I looked down at myself. I'd fallen on my bed in my dirty petticoat. The mud had dried, of course, but it looked awful. I turned in confusion and put my hands to my head, which was throbbing. "There isn't time to change. What'll I do?"

"Just wash your face and fix your hair," David advised solemnly. "Brush yourself off. The later you are, the more time they have to think. Jem, watch yourself with Reid. Mother and Father think the sun rises and sets with him."

"I know that, David."

"And take my advice and don't mention the war. That sets them off faster than anything."

Candlelight glowed softly in Father's study, reflecting on the bound books and soft draperies. Father was leaning back in his chair behind his desk, his legs stretched out, smoking his clay pipe. A goblet of wine was on his desk and another on the small table a few feet away where John Reid sat. They were talking in soft tones when I went in. My father was even smiling.

He saw me and sobered, pulled his legs in, and beckoned me toward him. "Jemima."

I ventured farther into the room. The candlelight and shadows played across John Reid's face, adding a quality of maturity I had never noticed before. He stood, inclined his head, and said my name politely, then flipped his coat-tails and sat again, his face betraying nothing.

Father puffed his pipe, ruminating. "How are you feeling, Jemima?"

"I'm all right, Father. Other than my head hurting."

"You had a fall. Was your head injured?"

"No. I fell on my hand. The Indian women at Grand-father's bandaged it."

"Let me see."

I went to him and he examined the wrist. "It looks fine. No swelling. The Indian women know their medicine. You look worse for wear, though."

"I'm sorry about the way I look, Father. I fell asleep and didn't wake until David knocked. I didn't take the time to change."

He nodded. "Sit down."

I sat and he considered me. "It's been a bad day for all of us, Jem. It started early and it looks as if it will never end. I had a long meeting with the Committee of Safety, which took up most of my day. You know how important those meetings have become these days."

I didn't think he should be discussing the Committee of Safety in front of John Reid, but I said nothing.

"And then I came home just before supper to find your mother completely distraught. Jemima, this has been one of the worst days of your mother's life, with Dan leaving. And you have added to her heartache."

It sounded awful when he said it that way, and there was

nothing I could add to it or detract from it to make it sound any better.

"Your behavior, from this morning on, has been disgraceful. I won't go into detail and categorize your sins. We're all tired and you know what they are. Sufficient to say that it seems almost beyond anyone's ability to make a proper young lady of you."

The clock on the mantel ticked. John Reid did not look at me.

"Mr. Reid here has attempted for two years to give you an education as befits a young woman of your station in life. You have tried his soul to the utmost. I don't know how he has kept his temper with you."

He hadn't. He'd lost it on more than one occasion, but I knew better than to say so.

"War is coming, Jem. With my work with the Committee and keeping the shop and your mother's work with her sewing for the army, we haven't time to worry where you have run off to next or what new ways you have come up with to disgrace yourself."

I was sure he was talking about my kissing Raymond Moore, and I prayed he wouldn't take it into his head to discuss that now. He didn't.

"When Rebeckah suggested this afternoon that you go to Philadelphia with her, your mother was sorely tempted to say yes. Lucy might be packing your bags now if it were not for Mr. Reid. He insists on trying again with you. So your mother and I have agreed."

"Thank you, Father."

"Don't thank me. If anyone deserves thanks, it's John Reid. But you stay only on the condition that you apply yourself to your lessons with diligence and attempt to control that wild nature of yours. Lessons will be five afternoons a week now instead of three. You are to be on time, be presentable, and behave in a well-bred and amiable manner. Now, John, suppose you tell her what lessons you have planned."

John Reid nodded cordially to my father and got up. "There will be added instruction in penmanship, as you requested, Jemima, and a more intense study of French and Latin. And sums. There will also be instructions in etiquette, which your father felt you could use. And I've added geography."

"Geography?" It sounded awful.

"This isn't the usual education for a young lady," my father said, "but your mother and I want more for you than just needlework and dancing. The times are changing, Jemima. As we struggle to preserve our freedoms, we must also have the moral clarity and education to handle those freedoms. Your mother and I want you prepared for the future."

"Yes, Father."

"You have an excellent tutor in John Reid. With his education at Harvard College, you have the best. If you ruin this chance, if Reid once comes to me with the complaint that you've run off or flouted his authority, you'll go to Philadelphia. To live with Rebeckah and Grandfather Henshaw and mingle with their Tory friends. Is that what you want?"

"No, sir." How my father could overlook the fact that a Tory was to have the job of teaching me the moral clarity to handle our future freedoms was beyond me. The situation would have been humorous, had I not been so tired.

"I was going to take Bleu away to punish you," he went on, "but John suggested I allow you to keep him. When your grandfather gave you that horse, he gave you a certain amount of freedom. And you have abused it. It's a terrible thing to abuse freedom, don't you agree?"

"Oh yes, Father!" Take Bleu? My heart would break, surely.

"The most important thing we're going to have to learn, if we win our freedom in these colonies, is to handle it properly. Your generation will have to learn that, Jem, and teach it to the next one. So Reid thought it best that you keep your horse. It is his belief that you don't teach freedom by taking it away."

I stared openly at John Reid, but he was looking down into his goblet of wine. What did a Tory know about freedom? To be sure, I had never heard him argue with my parents about his feeling of allegiance to the Crown. But that was only because it was Father's rule never to argue politics with old friends who happened to be Tories.

"At the first provocation, though, John has my permission to send Bleu back to Otter Hall."

So that was it. Reid had convinced Father I was to keep Bleu only so he could have that edge of power over me. And he'd covered it all over with talk about freedom!

"Go to bed now, Jem. Have Lucy give you some supper first and a cold compress for that head. Say good night to John."

"Good night, Mr. Reid."

He stood and did his little half bow. "Good night, Jemima. I'm sure we'll work well together from now on."

"Oh, Jemima, how did you find your grandfather?" Father asked.

I stopped at the door. "He was fine."

"I hear Canoe escorted you back to town."

"Yes."

"You had a chance to talk to him, then. What did you talk about?"

I hesitated, remembering the delicate situation between Father and Canoe.

"Come, come, Jemima. We've all heard the rumors concerning Canoe. It's always been to your credit that you have gone out of your way to be nice to him."

I glowed. I couldn't remember the last time my father had praised me. "He told me about his boyhood in Canada."

"Ah, a most interesting boyhood. There's a fine bit of education for you, John."

"I'd like to hear about it someday," Reid said earnestly.

"He told me how Indian children are raised. And how they are never punished."

Father looked at me over his spectacles. "Are you telling me you don't think you should be punished?"

"I'm only telling you what Canoe told me. Goodness, you asked."

He scowled. "I sense impudence, Jemima. I hope it wasn't intended."

"Oh no, Father."

I'd displeased him. I saw John Reid scowl at me and shake his head. I hadn't wanted to do that. For all my father's threats, he was a patient and good parent. I felt bad and stood, hoping he would invite me to kiss him good night. I yearned for him to take me in his arms.

"Don't forget your prayers, Jemima. Lessons will begin in a week. By that time your wrist should be back to normal and John Reid will have had time to prepare his course of study." He smiled kindly, but there was no invitation in the smile. I turned and left.

# CHAPTER

## *14*

When I reported to John Reid for my lessons a week later, there was an old inventory book of Father's on the round table in the middle of his study. I marched into the room and went immediately to the table where my mother's silver coffee service sat. I had just come in from riding Bleu and was numb with cold. It had been two hours since my noon meal and I was also starving.

I took off my cloak and threw it on a chair and reached for a piece of cold meat that was laid out on the silver tray next to Lucy's pumpkin bread and some dried fruit.

"Put it back."

I had the meat in my hand, halfway to my mouth. "What?"

John Reid was sitting languidly in a chair next to the fire going through some of his papers. He didn't bother to get up or even to look at me. "I said put it back. Barbarians eat with their hands. You wouldn't dare do that at your parents' table. And barbarians make such an entrance, clomping in with muddied shoes and throwing their clothes about. Put the meat back. You'll eat when given permission."

I put the meat down, too startled to do otherwise. In the

past he had commented once or twice on my unruly manners but never attempted to do anything about them. "It's my mother's food. And her coffee and her silver service that was made by Paul Revere and that she bought in Boston from a Tory who needed money."

"Go back outside and come in again. And this time come in quietly. And curtsy when you enter the room. Then pick up your cloak and hang it up properly."

"Well, I never! If you're going to be such an overbearing..."

He looked at me. "I am going to be overbearing. You were about to say?"

"I was about to say that only prissy girls from Miss Rodger's curtsy."

"Like Betsy Moore?"

"No, of course not. But—"

"Betsy Moore is a lady. And your brother Daniel is a gentleman, as befits his rank of officer in the Continental army. He wouldn't have any less than a true lady for a wife. You'll be a spinster at the rate you're going."

"And that's the way I'll stay if a man likes manners before he likes me."

He threw his head back and laughed. "You'll be a lady if I have anything to say about it. And you'll marry if I have to marry you myself."

"I'd sooner die!"

He sobered. "Go out and come in again, Jemima. We don't start lessons until you do."

I stomped out. Again I entered, more quietly, and stood looking at him.

"You know how to curtsy. I've seen you do it when you wanted something from your grandfather Henshaw. Can you do it for me?"

I screwed my face up in distaste and curtsied. He regarded me with a penetrating gaze that disquieted me. "Your head and shoulders could be held higher, but it will do for now."

"How do you know so much about it?"

"I've been in the company of a few fine ladies in my time."

"Like my sister, Rebeckah?"

Again he scowled. "You will kindly refrain from ever mentioning Rebeckah to me again. Is that understood?"

I nodded my head numbly.

"And when I speak to you, I expect a proper answer. Yes, sir. Or yes, Mr. Reid. Either will do, but I expect an answer. Well?"

"Yes, sir."

"Now pick up the cloak and hang it properly on the peg, and then you may eat."

He took a plate and arranged some meat and bread on it for me, pulled out my chair, and poured me some coffee. I sat. He sat opposite me, sipping his own coffee and watching me. "Don't stuff your mouth like that. And sit up straight. How you got to be fifteen with such horrendous manners is beyond me."

"I'll be sixteen in March."

"So you will. But sixteen or not, a properly brought-up Christian young woman does not kiss a man in public. Not even if she's betrothed to him."

I felt myself blushing. "What business is it of yours if I kissed Raymond Moore?"

"It comes under the heading of moral clarity, which I am supposed to be teaching you."

"Father was talking about moral clarity to handle freedom."

"Exactly. Freedom. And your constant misuse of it."

"That's not the freedom Father meant, Mr. Reid."

"I know the kind of freedom your father was talking about. And it starts with everyday life and entails great responsibility."

"Then you do admit that we'll win our freedom in these colonies."

"This has nothing to do with politics."

"Mr. Reid, how can you be so close to my parents and not see that we're right in our desire for self-government?"

"Jemima, I will not discuss politics with you. That subject, along with Rebeckah, is forbidden."

"Daniel is your friend, and he's off fighting a war."

"That's Daniel's choice."

"How can you be content to be a schoolmaster when so many people you know are fighting?"

"When the time comes, I'll offer my services. But I'm confident the rebellion will be crushed before then."

"Washington still has the British penned up in Boston. They're short of provisions and very miserable. That doesn't sound like we're being crushed."

"I'll hear no more about it. War has come to the colonies, unfortunately. It has torn apart the loyalties of everyone in Trenton. Since we are in the direct route between New York and Philadelphia, choices will have to be made by good men here, whether Tory or Patriot. Those choices are not easily made. Some of the most influential men in town will soon be throwing their fortunes in with the Crown. Lawyers, like Isaac Allen and Daniel Coxe; our high sheriff, John Barnes; and iron manufacturers, like Sam Henry. All good Americans."

"And then there's my father."

"Yes. Fortunately, he respects my position, the same as he respects that of Reverend Panton. But that is neither here nor there to you. You have lessons to learn. And no matter what goes on outside this room in the next few months, you will learn them. This is your war, Jemima Emerson"—he rapped the table—"and I am the enemy you must deal with. Now let's get started."

He got up to remove the silver tray, and as he did I noticed a letter on it. "What's this?" I picked it up.

He held out his hand. "Your lessons first."

"It's for me! It's from Raymond Moore and it's for me and you've kept it from me!"

"The letter is to be read after your lessons. Now please hand it over."

"I won't."

He set the tray down across the room, came back, and held out his hand. Our eyes met. "Give me the letter."

I flung it down on the table. It missed and fell to the floor. He closed his eyes. "Pick it up."

"Pick it up yourself."

He did so. Then he stood for a moment, turning the letter over and over. "You're determined to push me to the limit today, aren't you? Very well." He strode over to the fireplace. I saw his intentions immediately, ran across the room, and grabbed the sleeve of his coat. "Please, Mr. Reid."

"Please? You've suddenly found your manners? Jemima, I have no intention of entering into battle with you every time I come into this room." He made a move toward the fire.

"No!" I grabbed his sleeve again.

"Does Raymond Moore mean that much to you?"

"I promised to write to him. Isn't it also part of being a lady, to keep one's word?"

"You're very clever, Jemima. And how will you behave in the future if I don't burn the letter?"

"Most proper. Oh, I will."

"And is that a promise you'll keep to me?"

"Yes, sir."

He smiled. "Well, that's better. If Raymond Moore's letters work such wonders, I think I'll have them all given to me first. Then you'll get them, after lessons. Tonight you may compose a reply to this one and let me read it tomorrow, so I can make sure your penmanship is in order. Now let's get down to business."

He was beastly and I hated him. We did geography and French and Latin and sums for four hours while Raymond's letter sat between us. Then he set down Father's old inventory book in front of me in the proper writing position. His hands were very clean, and when his coat fell open I could see how white his shirt was. He smelled of soap and tobacco, like my father, which is all I could say to recommend him.

Oh, he knew he was handsome, all right. He strutted about the room when he lectured on geography or listened to my French and Latin pronunciation, ever aware of the breadth of his shoulders under his well-cut coat and the six feet of height that nature had blessed him with.

"Remember the correct posture for good writing," he said, adjusting the inventory book. "Does your wrist hurt? Can you manage?"

"No."

"No, you can't manage? Or no, the wrist doesn't hurt? What did I just say about giving proper answers?"

"No, sir, the wrist doesn't hurt. I can manage."

"Good." He filled his cup with coffee and took his papers to my father's desk, where he stretched his long legs out in front of him. I started to write, thinking that I ought to mention to Father not to keep any papers from his Committee of Safety work on his desk. I wrote:

Six pairs of boys' mitts. Two dozen sets of silver-plated shoe buckles. Three dozen fine-tooth combs. Fourteen yards of superfine brown broadcloth. Twenty-five yards of buckram. Eleven dozen stay hooks. Two boxes of scented soaps (one doz. in each box). Eleven dozen knitting needles. Twenty razors. Three dozen black silk handkerchiefs. Seventeen yards of plain gauze. Two cases of earthenware. A gross of thimbles. Two boxes of...

Oh, I'd ruined it! I'd ruined it! I leaned back in my chair to rest. My head was aching. John Reid was reading, taking no notice of me, going through those precious papers of his. I closed my eyes for a moment. When I opened them to look around the familiar room, I realized that his birch rod was not in its usual spot behind the door.

"Have you finished?"

"No, I've ruined it with spilled ink three times already. I'm never going to be able to do it right."

He came over to examine my work. "You're doing fine."

"I'm not. My writing is terrible."

"It will improve if you practice enough."

"I don't believe you. I'm sure there are certain things in life I'll never be able to do."

He sat down opposite me at the table. "Jemima, if it helps you, we all feel that way sometimes. Dan told me before he left that he hoped he had the sense of honor to uphold his rank, to keep his word and demand the same of others. Your father confides in me often of his fear that he won't raise his family properly. In three weeks I go off on a journey to do something that I hope I can have the courage and the wits to do right."

"You're going away?"

"I must go to Boston again."

"What's in Boston? Nothing but Tories. Are you going to see them?"

"It has something to do with my father's estate."

Mother had said something about his having property that had to be settled, but I hadn't known it was in Boston.

"Why do you need wits and courage to inherit property?"

"You do if others are trying to cheat you out of it."

"Oh." But somehow I sensed he was lying about his reasons for going to Boston.

"I'll have your course of study outlined for you so you can still do your lessons every day. And heaven help you if they aren't completed when I return. Jemima, are you paying attention to me? What are you staring at in the corner?"

"You didn't bring your birch rod today, Mr. Reid."

"No, I didn't. Somehow I didn't think I'd need to bring it anymore."

"Mother said you've never used it on anyone. Is that true?"

"Your mother told you that? Well, then, it's no wonder I was having such trouble controlling you. No, I've never used it on anyone. But my students don't know that. And as long as they don't, they behave. Now you know my little secret. Will you give me away to my students?"

"No, sir."

"And why?"

"Because if I do, they'll be unruly and you'll be provoked when you come to teach me. And then I'll suffer."

He smiled. "We are beginning to understand each other, Jemima. Come, now. Let's finish the penmanship."

# CHAPTER

## *15*

John Reid left for Boston in the middle of February and was back before the middle of March. I spent time every day in Father's study with my lessons, but it was difficult to keep at them on my own. I was lonely and would have preferred even Reid's stern presence to the silence in the room, broken only by the crackling fire and occasional footsteps in the hall. I was easily distracted. A few times Betsy Moore came to call, bringing a book and promising Mama that she would sit and read or hear my French. But we ended up talking. And then Hannah Fry, one of the women in Mama's Society for the Promotion of Industry and Frugality, with whom I sewed for the army twice a week, gave me a novel to read and I spent a lot of time with that. It was reading, after all, wasn't it?

I received another letter from Raymond Moore.

> Dear Jemima,
>     We travel to the north more and more and since this is the first time I have been away from home I note, with much interest, the changes in scenery.

I am enjoying the February thaw. The men have received me well into their midst, and, although they do taunt me, it is all in good spirits and they treat me as a comrade in arms. Thy brother is most esteemed by the men and I am fortunate to serve under him. And to have the prayers and good wishes of his sister, whom I hold in highest regard. I keep thy letter and read it every night by the fire. Thy memory burns within me as brightly as the flame in front of my eyes.

> Thy dear friend,
> Raymond Moore

I was glad that John Reid was away and unable to see the response I composed in return, for I took the opportunity to pour my heart out to Raymond before Reid would once again be reading my letters.

A letter came from Daniel:

Dear Jemima,

I'm glad to know your lessons go well and you have reached some accord with John Reid. I have learned very much about the men under me and they have become close to me. I pray every night that I can behave with humanity and consideration toward them and with conduct that befits an officer. Already on this trip one man in my company has died and was buried with the whole Regiment and chaplain attending. Afterward, ten of my men fired three rounds over his grave. I have already engaged in one court-martial, as another of my men was tried for desertion, drunkenness and disobedience. He was sentenced to twenty-five lashes.

But most of them fulfill the trust I have in them. Pray for me, that I may serve my country with fidelity.

> Your affectionate brother,
> Dan

On the twelfth of March John Reid came home.

I was in the upstairs hall when I heard a horseman ride into our stable yard in back of the house. I ran to the window to see who it was.

I recognized the horse, Star, but not the man who dismounted. He wore a rifle frock, much like one of Dan's regulars, frontier leggings, and a wide-brimmed hat pinned up on one side and decorated with a turkey feather. And he carried a long musket. As I watched him hand the reins to Cornelius and dislodge his saddlebags, he turned in the direction of the house, saw me at the window, and waved.

I had always considered John Reid somewhat of a dandy, for I'd never seen him dressed in anything but his finest-cut coat and breeches with his hair tied in a perfect queue. Now he looked like a backwoodsman. He had a beard, and if not for the horse I wouldn't have recognized him. I knew he'd taken Star as far as New York and left her there with friends and taken a carriage the rest of the way to Boston.

You would think the Prodigal Son in the Bible had returned, the way Mother and Father carried on.

"John, we're so happy your mission was a success," Mother was saying as I walked into the parlor. Father was serving brandy, and John Reid stood in front of the fire.

"Jemima." He bowed, and I stared at the tall, tanned figure in the rifle frock with a leather belt cinching the lean waist, from which hung a sheathed hunting knife. Surely this was not my tutor! But it was. He straightened up, and I saw beyond the growth of beard and sunburned face to the intense brown eyes twinkling mischievously at me. "You look well. It seems you've grown an inch taller in my absence."

I curtsied. "Hello, Mr. Reid. I was about to say how different you look."

"A fine mess is what I look. Have you been doing your lessons?"

But I could only stare, speechless. "Every day, John," Mother said.

"And her behavior?" He smiled at Father.

"We have no complaints," Father said. "Jem has been studying religiously. And she's been helping Sarah with the sewing for the army."

"Good." He reached into his saddlebags and brought out gifts—a book for Mother, some tobacco from Boston for Father, and a hunting knife for David.

"He'll be home for supper, John," Father said. "I hope you can join us."

Reid ran his hand over his face. "If Lucy could supply me with some hot water for washing and a shave. I have a clean shirt in my haversack." And then he handed me a packet. "To go with that beautiful blue dress," he said.

I opened it to find three hair ribbons, one blue, one lavender, and one yellow. I fingered them lovingly, for they were much finer than the ones Father had in his shop. When I looked up, I saw him studying me with satisfaction. I could barely find my voice to thank him, for something in his gaze disquieted me. "I'll see you in the study after supper to look at your work," he said firmly as he picked up his things. "Let's hope it's all in order."

I trembled, watching him take his leave of the room. I

had forgotten what it was like to have him in the same room with me, and now he was back, more arrogant than ever, filling the house with his presence.

"This French is not complete, Jemima. I left more than this for you to translate."

John Reid's shadow slanted against the wall in the candlelight as he stood over Father's desk examining my work. He had shaved and tied his hair back in a queue. But instead of his usual coat and waistcoat he wore a clean white shirt and a black silk stock at the collar. His sleeves were rolled up, revealing muscular arms.

"Well?" he looked at me. "Why is the French incomplete?"

"I did as well as I could without assistance."

He nodded and went through my sums. "These seem all right, although I can detect some errors upon a glance. Have you read all your Shakespeare?"

"No, sir."

"And why? Your mother said you spent the required hours each day studying. Or were you in here writing to Raymond Moore?"

"I've only written him two letters in your absence. I did a lot of reading."

"But not Shakespeare? Or the Milton or Dryden I assigned?"

"No, sir."

"What, then? Come on, out with it."

"Henry Fielding."

"A novel?" He scowled in disbelief, for novels were looked upon as frivolous and time-wasting. "Where did you get it?"

"From one of the women in Mama's Society."

"Do you have it still?"

"Yes, Mr. Reid."

"Then get it for me, please." His face was white with anger, even under his sunburn.

"It isn't my book. I have to return it."

"Will you get it for me, please?"

I went to Father's bookshelves, where I had hidden the book behind some others, and gave it to him.

"*Tom Jones!* Romantic nonsense! Whose is it?"

"Mrs. Fry's."

"So this is what you've been doing while you told your parents you were studying. What do you think they would say about this?"

"Will you tell them?"

He set the book down. "There is no need to. I'm capable of handling this myself. The first thing I'll do is return the book to Mrs. Fry."

"But I haven't finished it yet!"

"And you won't, either. As your tutor it's my job to guide your reading habits."

"But that's not fair! You read what you want! And while you were off in Boston, enjoying yourself with your Tory friends, I had to sit here and read dry old Milton and Dryden. I'd rather read *Poor Richard's Almanac*! Benjamin Franklin makes more sense! Do you have any idea what it's like to sit here alone, day after day?"

"I take it you missed me, then."

I only glared at him in response.

He smiled, but it was not kindly. "You'll go back to reading Shakespeare and Milton and Dryden tomorrow, in double doses. And for your wasting of time and deception, I'm taking Bleu away from you for two weeks. You're not even to exercise him. Cornelius can do that."

The unfairness of his punishment brought tears to my eyes. I looked forward each day to my winter rides on Bleu. "I hate you, Mr. Reid. And I'll find a way of getting back at you!"

The smile quickly faded from his lips. He looked at me fully and deliberately for a long moment, but with such confusion and pain in his eyes that it frightened me. Then he looked silently at my work on the desk. I waited. I saw the muscle in his jaw twitch, but I could not see much else, for his eyes were hidden.

"I shall look forward to the challenge, Jemima." He did not raise his head as he answered, and he sounded more sad than angry.

I stood looking at him, satisfied that my intent to hurt had found its mark, but confused as to why. Certainly I had told him before that I hated him. Usually he would just laugh and pull my hair as he walked by my chair and say something clever.

"Do you have any other kind sentiments you wish to impart to me at the moment, Jemima?"

"No, sir."

"Then you may go."

I left. Still he would not look at me.

The next morning I awoke with an aching, stuffed head. I'd ridden Bleu to my heart's content in John Reid's absence, and the cold that had been threatening me the last day or so came with a vengeance. With the exception of measles, I had always enjoyed the best of health, so much so that Mother had often remarked that it was almost scandalous for a girl to be so robust. But that afternoon I dragged myself to lessons, where I managed to stay attentive for two hours. John Reid was especially demanding, but after two hours

I felt as if my head were filled with goose down, and I couldn't even form my answers properly. When I had, twice in a row, given him an incorrect answer in geography, he slammed his book down on the table in a way that echoed most unpleasantly in my head.

"Jemima Emerson, do you provoke me intentionally because I've taken your horse away from you? Or have you become more adept at stupidity in my absence?"

"No, sir." But I could not even comprehend the question.

He scowled, no doubt suspecting impudence. "No, sir, what?"

I shook my head numbly.

"What's wrong with you?"

"I think I'm not feeling very well."

He got up and came to scowl over me. I leaned back in my chair, clutching my book, but he reached out and put a hand on my forehead as gently and practiced as Mama would have done. Then he took my book from me. "Go and tell your mama that I said you have a fever and you're to be put to bed. There will be no lessons tomorrow. In heaven's name, child, why didn't you tell me?"

For two days I lay in bed, pampered by Mama and Lucy, feverish and sleeping and giddy-headed. On the third day the fever left, although I was sneezing and sniffling. The March weather had turned cold and blustery again, so Mama said I could sit by the fire in the parlor, where it was warmer than my room. I was curled up with a quilt around me, in the afternoon, trying to concentrate on some Milton, as Mama had suggested, when someone came across the carpet. I looked up to see John Reid in boots, breeches, his rough brown cloak, and a tricorn hat. He took the hat off and gave his little half bow. "I trust you're feeling better?"

"Yes, sir." He looked very healthy, and he brought in the freshness of the outdoors with him.

"Your mama says I may visit if I don't tire or berate you. I have promised to do neither." He unfastened the cloak and put it carefully over a chair, also setting down his hat and a small package. "Do you mind my presence?"

"No, Mr. Reid."

At that moment Lucy came in with Mama's silver coffee service and some delicious-smelling corn bread. "Thank you, Lucy." Reid turned from warming his hands by the fire and poured two cups of coffee. "I'm told that you haven't been eating. You must if you want to get well, you know."

"I feel as if I could eat some of that corn bread."

"Good." He buttered a piece and set it down with the coffee on a table next to me. He smiled wryly. "What are you reading now? Another contraband novel?"

I blushed and shook my head no. He took the book from my hands, saw what it was, and raised his eyebrows in amusement. "You are voluntarily reading Milton?"

"Mama said I should try to make up for lost time."

"We'll do that when you get well, I can promise you." He put sugar and cream in his coffee and sat down in a nearby chair. "I've been riding Bleu."

Oh, and was he here to tease me, then? How cruel!

"He needed the run. And since you were indisposed..."

"I wouldn't be able to ride him even if I were well."

"Yes, that's true. But David has offered to take him out on the days I can't." Again the wry smile. "Come, now, don't pout. You openly provoked me. What else was I to do?"

I raised my chin defiantly. "You know how much I enjoy riding."

"Yes, I do. And I can understand why. Bleu's a marvelous

horse. When these two weeks are up, we'll go for a ride, you and I, to Otter Hall. Would you like that?"

"Yes, sir." But I would not look at him.

He finished his coffee and stood up. "I sense that was more a dutiful reply than anything. And I also sense that I am tiring you. I shan't force you to ride with me, Jemima." He put on his cloak, then picked up the small package he had brought and set it in my lap.

"What is it?" I looked up at him.

"A little something to . . . make up for the book I took away from you."

I undid the brown paper. It was a slender, richly bound book with gilt edges. I opened it. *The Love Sonnets of William Shakespeare.*

"Oh!" I exclaimed. The paper was delicate and the cover was made of rich leather. Inside he'd written something: "Some romantic nonsense to fill your leisure hours until you can ride your horse again. Your devoted tutor, John Reid."

I felt a stab of poignancy. The color rose to my face as if the fever had returned. But when I looked up to stammer my thanks, I could only stare at him, tongue-tied. For his look had changed to one of such troubled intensity as he contemplated me that I became twice as confused. Then, in an instant, he clapped the tricorn hat on his head. "Be well, Jemima," he said. And in a whirl of brown cloak he turned and was gone from the room.

But I had not thanked him. All afternoon I sat by the fire with the book in my hand, examining it, going over his written words and seeing him standing there, waiting for me to acknowledge the gesture, then turning on his heel and leaving. The recollection of how he'd stood there and the look on his face troubled me. For I had seen, in that instant, a John Reid I had never seen before. There was uncertainty in his eyes, a question where uncertainties and questions had never shown before. Was the fever still with me? Had I imagined it? Had he been waiting for something from me? And what? Forgiveness? Yes, that, but more. Oh, my head ached again thinking on it. I closed my eyes and slept with the book still in my hands.

On the fifth day, when Mama said I was well enough to go back to my lessons, I approached them with great apprehension.

"Ah, you're well again, Jemima." John Reid looked up from the book he was reading in front of the fire.

"Yes, sir, I'm better."

"Good, we have a lot of catching up to do."

"Mr. Reid, may I say something first?"

"Yes, of course."

I twisted the corner of the apron that Mama always made me wear to lessons because I stained myself so with ink. "I want to . . . to thank you for . . . for the book of poetry."

He nodded, but the look in his eyes was veiled. "You're quite welcome. Come now, let's get to work."

He never asked me about the book again. Indeed, it was as if he had never given it to me, never written those words inside it. Our sessions progressed as always, except that he was now twice as demanding, trying to make up for lost time. I began to wonder, under hours of grueling study, when my head seemed to burst from fatigue and my fingers became stiff from writing, if I had not imagined the whole episode in my fever.

But I knew I hadn't, for I was reading the love sonnets every day and enjoying them so much that I didn't ache with longing to ride Bleu. Not as much as I'd thought I would, anyway. Oh, I visited Bleu in the barn each day and talked to him and gave him some dried apple, but I was so tired that I couldn't have ridden him even if I'd been allowed to.

I was under a strain, that was the heart of the matter. I didn't know how to act with John Reid. His kindness had thrown me off balance. It's quite one thing, after all, to have someone be mean to you and another to have that person suddenly exhibit kindness. I found it most disconcerting. I had always known where I stood with him, and now I did not.

But all this didn't change the fact that I still intended to get back at him for taking my novel and Bleu away. It was a matter of pride that I do so. And he expected me to, I was sure of it.

One night when he was having supper with us, as he seemed to be doing all the time lately, my father looked at him across the table. "Jem looks pale, John. Are you sure you aren't bearing down too hard with the studies?"

"Jemima wasted quite a bit of time while I was away, contrary to what she told you. And then with her sickness . . . we're trying to make up for it."

"You haven't been riding your horse, Jem," Mama said. "Are you sure you're fully recovered?"

From across the table John Reid caught my eye, warning me to be silent. I preferred it that way, for if Father found out about my deception and novel reading, it would be worse than having only my tutor know.

"I'm fine, Mama."

"Jem is being punished," John Reid said patiently. "I took Bleu away from her for two weeks."

"For what?" Father asked.

He took a sip of wine. "For insubordination," he said

simply. The tone of his voice was polite but indicated he did not wish to elaborate. Thank goodness my parents changed the subject.

Before the two weeks were up we received word from a messenger who rode into town that the British had evacuated Boston on the seventeenth of March. Washington, strengthened by cannon and mortars that Colonel Henry Knox had brought down from Fort Ticonderoga by sled, moved to Dorchester Heights, south of the city. Forced to either fight or leave, British General William Howe chose to leave and sailed out of Boston. It was reported that Washington's army was on the way to New York City.

I couldn't wait to tell John Reid about it and see his face. I found him waiting for me in Father's study.

"You're late, Jemima," he said, looking up from his papers.

I remembered to curtsy. "I was in Father's shop. People have been coming in all morning and lingering to talk about the news."

"Oh? What news is that?"

"Haven't you heard? General Howe has evacuated Boston."

"Oh, that, yes. I heard earlier this morning."

"What a victory for Washington! Howe left rather than fight! Don't you think it's wonderful?"

"Anything is wonderful that means an end to war and an attempt at reconciliation."

"This has nothing to do with reconciliation. Howe simply fled under Washington's guns!" Now he was being the Tory, and that made me angry. "It's too bad you weren't there. You might have fled with him."

"Do you really wish I had been there, Jemima?" He was

looking down at his papers as he said it, but then he raised his eyes. And once again he was looking at me as he had done the day he'd given me the book, with a gaze I can only describe as troubled intensity.

"I . . . well, I . . . no, sir, I didn't exactly mean that. What I meant was . . ."

"Why don't we just get on with lessons," he said, smiling wryly, "and leave General Howe to his own problems?"

# CHAPTER

## *16*

I turned sixteen on the thirtieth of March, and Lucy and Mother were planning a supper in my honor. Mother had found time in the middle of her sewing for the army and her letter writing to make me a new English gown of printed fabric Father had imported from France months back. It was an arrangement of brown and red and blue flowers on a background the color of fresh cream, and I felt very grown up in it.

"You look so lovely, Jem," Mother said as I tried the gown on.

"Am I as pretty as Rebeckah?"

"Prettier. And I have it on the authority of John Reid."

"Well, I don't want to be pretty if he says so." I turned away. I had caught Reid looking at me quite a lot lately, with that same strange intentness he'd exhibited the day he'd given me the book. It confused me, yet at the same time pleased me in ways I didn't want to think about. "Mama, why do you always bring John Reid up to me? You know I dislike him."

"Do you, Jem?" In the mirror I saw her lean her head

against mine. "I wonder if you are not just covering up something you can't face at the moment."

"Mama, you know I'm corresponding with Raymond Moore!"

She fussed with my gown. "Well, at least you're talking about young men this year. Last year when your father wanted to make you a chest for your linen dowry, you wouldn't hear of it. Now he's made you a fine one for your birthday. We'll have to get started sewing your linens soon."

"Mama, there's time. And you have enough to do. You look tired as it is." It was true. She looked pale and thinner these days, but she had always been slender, with graceful hands. She was everywhere at once in the house, capable and serene. But now there were tired lines in her face that had nothing to do with the usual crinkles around her blue eyes.

She tucked the wisps of yellow hair under her neat cotten mobcap. "Yes, I am tired, Jem. But I must stay busy. It keeps me from worrying about Dan. And now David's talking about joining the local militia."

"He's only fourteen!"

"He'll be fifteen in a month, and he's tall enough for seventeen. We won't be able to keep him a merchant's apprentice long, with the war coming."

She would take this in stride too, as she took everything else—sending Dan off, sewing for the army, writing essays, teaching Lucy to read, running the house smoothly, making herbal concoctions for our medicine, and overseeing the cooking and the dye and soap making.

I hugged her. "I love you, Mama." She felt so fragile in my arms.

"My, what brought this on?"

"I just do. May I wear the dress for lessons today?"

"I thought you didn't care what John Reid thought of you. No, you may not. You come from lessons ink-stained. Wear your old petticoat and chemise and short gown. You may change later for supper."

I was startled to find John Reid waiting for me in the study, for I thought I was early. He was leaning over Father's desk, and I was halfway in the room before he saw me. He looked up, startled. His tanned face went ashen when he saw me. "Jemima, you're early."

"I didn't mean to startle you, Mr. Reid."

"I was engrossed in what I was doing." Hastily he covered the papers on the desk.

"Your correspondence seems to take up almost as much time as my mother's."

"I have many business dealings to wind up concerning my estate."

I had not curtsied and he had not noticed. "Will you be a very rich man when you are done?"

"Very rich indeed, Jemima, in spirit if not entirely in funds."

I could not understand his meaning. Reverend Panton talked about being rich in spirit. It was clergyman's talk, not the talk of a schoolmaster, and certainly not of a Tory! But what remained with me more than his remark was the ashen color of his face when I'd surprised him. Something was in those papers, I decided, that was far more important to him than the settling of an estate. I pretended innocence, however, and kept my voice cheerful. It was, after all, my birthday, and I teased him, sensing his discomfort at being surprised.

"I'm sixteen today, Mr. Reid. Now you have to treat me like a young lady."

"I've been trying to tell you for the last year to act like one, Jemima. You certainly look the part. If you think I haven't noticed, you're wrong. I'd be most happy to treat you that way if you would act accordingly."

In the middle of French Mother knocked on the open door. "John, I hate so to interrupt, but Cornelius is busy in the barn and Lucy is out to market, and I need help with the fire."

"Certainly, Sarah." He instructed me to read the next few pages of French and left. I listened to their footsteps receding down the hall. Then I dashed over to the desk, reached across it, and turned his papers around. One paper was lying on top of another one and had peculiar openings cut into it. I had never seen anything like it. There was nothing written on it. But the second paper underneath was a letter. I read it quickly, and it was only an ordinary letter from one of his Tory friends in Boston. Then I went back to the paper with the peculiar openings and couldn't resist placing it over the letter, for when it had lain on the desk, a few words had been visible through those openings.

I gasped at the result. What had first been just a letter was now a message! Only certain words showed through the holes in the top paper and my head reeled as I read them.

My dear sir:
    *General Howe has gone* from hence. The rebels imagined that he left for New York, but it was soon clear to us who remained that he planned to sail *to Halifax*. As I dispatch this the *word is out* that Howe was loath *to* fight *Washington*. Howe's ships lay, dropping anchor in the harbor for days, and *Washington* wondered what surprise and terror the British planned next. Then one fine morning

a signal fluttered from the British ships and their fleet *moved out* and turned—north!

Having previously concluded their next place of attack was New York, Washington had already sent *his riflemen and five infantry regiments* thither. He has need of supplies, I hear, as he goes *to New York*. The British have need of rest and a chance to reorganize.

The other news is that Congress has issued letters of marque to permit the outfitting of American privateers to prey on British shipping. It is *a job* Congress obviously feels must be done. I understand many American merchants are buying shares in profiteer ships. *You might consider* it yourself as it *should prove* to be *an excellent way to profit*. Many Americans, unscrupulous as it may sound, will profit from the share of captured merchandise. So much for *the Cause*. Should you *come to Boston*, I will assure *you*, you *will be needed* sorely to keep me company, for I am here alone in *this* city which has suffered the costs of war. I am sure that Howe will reorganize by *summer* and will make *plans* for his next attack with renewed fury. Many celebrations *are being made* in honor of Washington's victory at Boston, but I remain here with a small force, unsure and afraid *for the future*. You would laugh if you heard *Washington* talking of his *needs* and his fear of British *spies*. I wish you every success and remain your friend. . . .

I heard the sharp intake of my own breath as I read and reread the letter as it appeared through the openings of the paper on top of it.

My head reeled. What was to be made of it? What could be made of it except the truth? John Reid was a spy!

An American spy? But how could he be? He was an avowed Tory!

He didn't try to hide it, and the fact was known all through town. Several of Father's Patriot friends had already commented on the fact that my tutor was a Tory, but Father continued to defend him as the son of his best friend. I was so lost in thought that I did not hear Reid approach. My back was to the door, for I had reached across Father's desk to look at the papers. I cried out in terror as an ironlike hand gripped my wrist.

"Oh!" Fear surged through me as he whirled me around to face him. "So you're into my papers, are you? You deceiving little minx. I should have known better than to leave you alone in the room with them. Drop it."

But I refused. He tried to retrieve his paper with his free hand, but he didn't want to rip it. "Drop it!" he ordered savagely, and when I again refused he pulled me over to the door and kicked it shut with his foot.

It was Mama's rule that the door remain open always when he was tutoring me. It was only proper. Where was she now? In the kitchen, no doubt, preparing my birthday supper.

"Let me go!"

He brought his hand down on mine several times, slapping it sharply until I cried out in pain and released the paper, which fell to the floor. I stood nursing my poor hand as tears flowed down my face. Hastily he picked up his paper. Then, perceiving that I was about to flee, he grabbed me again. This time he pulled me by my wrist across the room and sat me down hard in a chair.

"What have you seen?"

"Nothing."

"Do you expect me to believe you? You lie!"

"No, I never read them. I mean I didn't understand—"

He took me by the shoulders and shook me. "You little fool! This is far more than a prank! My life is at stake here. If you read the letter, you know that by now! Did you read it? I want the truth. And if I think you're lying, I won't be easy on you, Jemima, I mean it. Try me if you will, but you'll be sorry if you do."

I believed him. His face was livid with anger and his eyes were blazing. He still gripped my shoulders. He would know if I lied, he always did. He was so angry, I believed him capable of anything.

"Yes," I said shakily.

"Yes, what?"

"Yes, sir, I read it."

"And did you understand what you read?"

I nodded my head yes. My heart was hammering inside me.

He released me and stepped back to survey me, standing with his hands on the hips of his breeches, the letter half crumpled in one hand. He was coatless, and I could see the rise and fall of his chest that was heaving in anger.

"Do you know how despicable a sneak is?"

A spy. He was a spy for the Americans! My head whirled in dizzy understanding as I looked up at him, standing in front of me, tall and lanky and broad shouldered, still tanned from his trip, his dark good looks spoiled by his anger.

"Answer me!" he snapped.

"Yes, sir."

"What have I taught you in these last two years about decency and honor? Nothing?"

"I thought—"

"You thought what?"

"I thought you were a Tory."

"And would that be reason to go into my private papers?"

"No. But you aren't a Tory. You're a Patriot, after all. You deceived me."

"I had to. It's part of my job. My life depends on it, can you understand that?"

"You mean—"

"I mean that I'll hang from the highest tree or the nearest gallows if the British find out. Would that please you? I know you hate me, so perhaps it would."

"Oh no, Mr. Reid . . . " I started to get up.

"Sit there!" he snapped. "You'll not leave that chair until I settle this and decide what's to be done about you." He started to pace the floor, once, twice, three times, in front of me. I watched him, seeing him as for the first time.

"Is that why you stayed in Boston last summer after Mama and Daniel came back?"

He cast me a dark glance and continued pacing.

"Daniel said that only spies and some travelers could get through."

Still he continued pacing.

"Mama won't like it if the door is shut."

"That door stays shut until I deal with you."

He was ever the schoolmaster.

"Is that why you went to Boston in February? You have no property in Boston, do you? You spied for Washington before he fortified Dorchester Heights!"

"Be quiet!"

"Did you meet Washington?"

He stopped pacing and glared at me. Then he pulled me to my feet, gripping my shoulders again. "In heaven's name, Jemima, do you know what it is that you say? This town is full of Tories! Must I live in fear that every time you step outside this house I am in danger of being reported to the British authorities?"

"I wouldn't report you, Mr. Reid. Please let me go. You're hurting me."

He realized that he was and released me. "You had no right to go into my papers. I've a mind to tell your father to birch you."

"Do my parents know?"

He looked at me. "Why do you think they've been so understanding of my so-called Tory philosophies?"

"And Daniel, too. That's why you two always had your heads together. Who else?"

"That's it. Except for you. And now my life isn't worth the King's shilling."

"Mr. Reid, I would never tell a soul. Why do think so little of me?"

"Because I know how little you think of me. Let's at least be honest. Honesty is one of your better qualities—at least it was until today."

"I'm sorry, Mr. Reid."

He turned to gaze at me, taking all of me in, down to my very soul, and it made me shudder. "I believe you are, Jemima. This time. But that doesn't help me or lull me into thinking that you wouldn't use this as an opportunity to either blackmail me into making life easier for you or to give me away."

"I wouldn't do that."

"You've been looking for the chance to get back at me for my strictness. Admit it."

I said nothing.

"Now you have your chance," he said bitterly.

"I don't feel that way anymore, Mr. Reid."

"Ha! Do you expect me to believe that?"

"Yes. Mostly I hated you because you were a Tory."

"Mostly you hated me because you plain hated me, Jemima. A few weeks ago, when you were ill, I attempted to make amends with you, and you would have none of it."

"I . . . I was ill," I stammered, "and I was caught off guard by your kindness and didn't know how to act. I cherish the book of poetry you gave me. I read it every day."

"You cherish the book I gave you, yet I can't trust you alone in the room with my papers." He smiled sardonically. "Come, now, Jemima, you dislike me intensely because of the way I've kept you under my thumb. It's become a challenge for you to constantly provoke me. Admit it."

"All right, but—"

"Exactly. So if I had a brain in my head, I'd save my skin by going directly to your father and advising him to ship you off to Philadelphia."

"I'd die in Philadelphia! And besides, Mama wouldn't let me go. She worries over Dan and told me today that David is wanting to join the militia. She wouldn't part with me."

"Let me tell you something, miss. Your parents would pack you off today if they thought I stood in danger of being hanged because of something you let slip, in innocence or not."

He was right. "So now it's up to me again. What shall I do with you this time?" He began pacing again. Despite his predicament, he seemed to be enjoying himself a little, watching me suffer.

"Philadelphia gets terribly hot in the summer," I said, "and there is always disease in the cities in summer. I would certainly die."

"You might well die from studying here with me the rest of the spring. I'll add science to your studies. It's not a pastime that females are generally fond of, but I must keep you busy. After I tell your father about this, I shall ask him to let you help him mornings in the shop. You know your sums, and his work with the Committee of Safety is increasing. That way I'd always know where you were and what you were up to. And you wouldn't have time to tell people what your hateful tutor is doing in his spare hours."

"I don't hate you. I think what you're doing is most wonderful."

"Spying is not wonderful, Jemima. My work is all secrecy. I'm on my own. If I'm caught, no one steps forward to help. Everyone despises what spies do. And I won't have you thinking it's wonderful. Or gossiping a word about it to anyone. Not David or Lucy, not even your parents. They never speak of it to me. And when you and I leave this room today, the discussion is closed forever between us. If you violate that trust, I'll be finished with you completely."

"You can trust me."

"That remains to be seen. You are sixteen today, but it's up to you to prove to me that you are a grownup. You can start proving it this evening at supper. There will be company, but you must pretend nothing has happened between us. I'll talk to your parents about it tomorrow. But tonight you will act polite and agreeable and give away nothing, or tomorrow I'll have your head, I can promise you that."

At supper, as I sat in my new gown at a table surrounded by friends and family, with John Reid dressed in his best dove-gray breeches and coat and whitest linen, it was as if our quarrel had never happened. He was the witty schoolmaster, reciting stories about the boys he taught each morning, the surrogate son to my parents, the cordial dinner guest, always attentive to my mother. He talked about hunting with David, discussed the merits of Miss Rodger's School with Mrs. Moore and Betsy, and entered into a lively discourse with Reverend Panton about the recent imprisonment of New Jersey's Tory governor Franklin. Once or twice he caught my eye in warm approval. I watched him in amazement. The man was an actor. He should have been in plays, and it was obvious that everyone was captivated by his dark good looks and debonair manner.

He gave me a book for my birthday called *Paradise Lost*. The look in his brown eyes as I opened it made me feel that the title was especially significant. And I was conscious, suddenly, of the scooped neckline of my gown and the way Mama had arranged my hair, with high curls that cascaded down the back of my neck. I felt my face go hot under his gaze.

Thankfully, Father got up to give a toast just then. Over the table laid with Mama's fine white linen and pewter and silver serving pieces, he stood, his spectacles resting on his finely chisled nose, his hair curling in wisps around his ears.

"These are not joyful times for any of us," he said, "but let us not discuss the war tonight. We drink to absent friends and family members and keep them in our hearts. I'm sure they would want us to be happy tonight in each other's company, and for my beautiful daughter, Jemima, who is sixteen years old today and a lovely young lady indeed."

"Hear, hear," I heard John Reid intone. My face burned all the more.

"Everyone does his part these days, no matter what road the good Lord has given us," Father continued. "No one knows what the future will bring, but I couldn't help overhearing some of our dear, faithful Lucy's philosophy a few times lately when there was some discussion about David joining the militia. Did I say discussion? It was more like heated argument."

Everyone laughed. He went on.

"During one of these discussions, I overheard Lucy mumbling, 'Time enough for drums.' 'What do you mean, Lucy?' I asked her. 'Drums on the battlefield,' she said; 'time enough for drums.'"

There was silence all around the table. "Well, tonight let us enjoy each other's company," Father finished. "There is time enough for drums."

# CHAPTER

## *17*

It was court week in Trenton. All up and down Queen Street there were wagons and gigs and sulkies. Since Trenton was the seat of Hunterdon County, the roads were lined with traffic. Lawyers stayed in town the entire week for court, which was good for business. The inns and public houses were always filled. Stagecoaches brought all kinds of people, while others came by horse and boat from New York and Philadelphia.

I looked down the long white pine counter to where my father was talking with a customer, a man in a powdered wig and fancy brocaded waistcoat. My father was exhausted already and it wasn't even noontime yet. It seemed like half the town had come in during the morning, needing new hats or sleeve buttons or razors or tobacco or snuff or watch chains.

"Nine other merchants besides yourself are involved," the man was saying.

"I'm not involved," my father told him. "I don't wish to hold shares in a privateer ship."

"I know it's a financial risk, James."

"Damnation, I'm not afraid of risk," my father said. "Life is a risk. So is marriage and being a Patriot. But I won't profit from the miseries of others. Now, it's going to be a long day, Andrew. Do you want your tobacco or don't you?"

"You know I do. You carry the best in town. We of the merchant community in Philadelphia have heard that elections for New Jersey's Third Provincial Congress are being held this week, James. The talk at the Indian King Tavern is that you will be elected as one of the deputies. You have our best wishes."

"I'll need them," Father said, "but I cannot discuss it. You understand."

"Of course. Will you be at the tavern tonight? It's the best place for hearing news and discussing politics."

"I'll try to be there, Andrew."

He left. I ran over to Father. "You didn't tell me about the Congress!"

"It's best not spoken of, Jem. We face many problems. There are heavy demands being put on New Jersey's military resources. We have a shortage of arms. In spite of our appeals to the Continental Congress, they refuse to supply us, yet we must assist both Pennsylvania and New York when they ask for battalions of minutemen for protection."

"But you said there is more and more feeling these days for independence."

"Hush. We don't say that word freely yet. Yes, there is. And I credit Tom Paine's little pamphlet for that. It's really roused people to our cause and made fence-sitters on the subject make up their minds." He patted the stack of *Common Sense* pamphlets that he kept on the counter. Everyone was talking about Tom Paine and his wonderful writings.

"But look here, if I do get elected to the Congress, I'll have to go to Burlington in June. Your mother will take my place in the shop while I'm away, but you will have to assist her."

"I will, Father, I promise."

"What is she promising now?" John Reid appeared in the doorway.

"Good morning, John. Or is it noon already? It is, by heaven. Lucy will be bringing my meal over in a minute. I can't leave the shop today. We're too busy. You'll be happy to know that Jem was indispensable to me this morning. I don't know what I would have done without her."

"Good, good." Reid picked up one of the pamphlets and laid down some coins. "I'll have one, sir. Jemima, I think it's time you read this. For its literary content, that is." He winked at my father. "I'm going to steal her from you now, James. Here, Jemima, you carry it. It wouldn't look right if I were carrying such Patriotic drivel."

It was the first time in the weeks since I had found out about his spying activities that he had ever referred to anything political. He still spoke like a Tory, although at that moment in jest. My father smiled at him as we walked out.

I followed him into the warm May sunshine. On the wooden walk outside my father's shop was a pile of goods tagged and boxed and ready to be taken to the river for shipment by barge to Philadelphia.

He paused. "Do you know what this is?"

Was this a lesson? It might be, for recently my education had been going beyond the boundaries of books. One fine April day a few weeks before, he had announced in the middle of my studies that we were going for a walk. We ended up going to the market in King Street for Mother. I loved to go to the market with Mother or Lucy, but with John Reid it was an adventure. He pointed out the farmers in their stalls, told me where they came from, and speculated on what profit they were making. Then he gave me some money and I purchased the fish, lemons, and nutmegs Mother had asked for, under his watchful eye. He bought a small sack of sweetmeats, and we ate them on the way home.

Now he was poking at the goods with his shoe. "This is the last shipment of goods your father will be sending to his friend Thomas Riche. Flour, pork, flax, seed, let's see what else . . . wigs, stoneware, and lumber. Your father has found out that Riche is shipping to the British. Do you know what that means?"

"It means my father has lost a very dear friend."

"It also means Riche won't be sending your father any more sugar, wine, salt, saltpeter, coffee, or molasses. And he'll miss having those items in his shop. The war has its price, Jemima, and we feel it more and more each day."

I matched his stride on the wooden walk to our front door, happy that he was talking to me as an equal. He'd done it most often over the last five weeks. I hadn't once referred to his spying; I'd worked in the shop every morning and sat with the utmost decorum and attention at lessons each afternoon. Only once in the last month did he have to scold me, and that was for gazing out the open window into the inviting April day.

In the wide entryway to our house he took off his tricorn hat and linen coat.

"Good day, Mr. Reid." Lucy came out of the study and gave him a quick curtsy. "Hello, Jemima," she said to me. She'd just left our noon meal in the study, where we ate every day after he came from his boys' school and I from the shop.

"A fine day it is, too," John Reid said, nodding to her.

Our midday meal had become a ritual. He would pull

out my chair and serve my food, and pour me some milk or cider, then serve himself. He might glance at the *Pennsylvania Gazette* that Lucy had set by his plate and ask about my morning in the shop. As I recited the morning's events, he would question me, making sure I understood why so-and-so would say such a thing or why the cost of coffee or sugar cones was rising or where my father's imports were coming from and how.

Occasionally he still corrected my speech or manners, and if I wanted to go anywhere, even to Betsy Moore's or Grandfather Emerson's, I had to ask his permission. It was only right, my father said, since I had taken it upon myself to go through his papers, and his life was more or less in my hands.

That day he didn't ask about the shop, however. "You didn't respond to Lucy," he said.

I looked at him, uncomprehending.

"She greeted you good day. You ignored her. I've noticed you do a lot of that with Lucy. Sometimes you are outright insulting to her."

"It's always been that way with Lucy and me."

"Why?"

I could give him no answer.

"I despise slavery," he said. "It's a loathsome practice, and someday we're going to pay for it in these colonies. It's one of the reasons I came late to the Cause. All that talk of liberty when we were keeping slaves."

"What made you change your mind?"

"When I went to Boston for Rebeckah's wedding and I saw the arrogance and pompous stupidity of the British troops there. I was loyal to the King until I saw his troops quartered in the houses and on the Commons. Mobs roamed the streets at night and refugees constantly streamed into the city. There were empty warehouses and British ships in the harbor, and everyone was hungry, it seemed. I went to Harvard College and I loved Boston. It broke my heart as much as seeing Rebeckah marry that British officer."

I was under his spell. He had never confided such things to me before. "So, when I found out spies were needed by Washington, I volunteered on the spot. But we were talking about your rudeness to Lucy. Your father plans to free her and Cornelius one day soon. I would like you to make an effort to be decent to her. I don't like it when you hurt people by being thoughtless or superior."

"All right, Mr. Reid, I'll try."

He smiled. "And when are you going to answer the latest letter from Raymond Moore? You've put it off for a week. Is there a reason?"

My heart became chilled, like a cold meatcake inside me. There was a reason, but how could I tell him? Raymond's letter suddenly seemed stilted and childish. I'd come to realize, under John Reid's tutelage, that I had grown much older and wiser. Raymond was just a childhood friend, and I was no longer a child.

But there was more, and my heart, the cold meatcake, was bursting for being unable to say it.

"Well?" he insisted.

"I don't know how to answer his last letter."

"Why?" His brown eyes scrutinized me.

"He . . ." I stammered it out, ". . . He's asked to court me when he comes home, and I don't want it."

He nodded, sipping his coffee. "Why don't you want to?"

"Well, goodness." I blushed. "I feel a great distance between us—not because he's away, but because I've grown up so and there is no common bond with us anymore."

"Don't you want to marry someday, Jemima?"

"Yes, sir, but not Raymond Moore."

"Who, then? Have you someone in mind? Your mother tells me you languish about the house and stare at nothing. She thought you were smitten with Raymond."

I did not know where to look. At my hands in my lap? Why wouldn't he stop staring at me? I worked my linen napkin between my fingers.

"Stop twisting your napkin in that distracting way and look at me," he said quietly.

I did. My eyes filled with tears as I raised them and looked full into the dear, familiar face of the man who had been my hated teacher, who had teased and tormented me and made me suffer. The man who had taken the trouble to teach me to curtsy correctly and hold my fork right, who had berated and shamed me into being a lady, even while he hammered French and Latin and geography into my head. We had made a long journey together. I knew I pleasured him, for I saw the way he looked at me when he thought I wasn't taking notice. Yet never once in our long hours together did he dishonor the faith my parents had in him by so much as touching my hand with his own.

He saw the anguish in my look and more. He got up. I thought I heard him murmur, "Dear God," as he turned away, but I couldn't be sure. He went to the window and stood with his back to me, looking out on the fine May afternoon.

"You must write to Raymond. You promised, and I'll not have you go back on your word."

"But—"

"No buts. He's far from home, waiting for your letters. You must not treat him the way Rebeckah treated me."

"I've angered you."

"Yes, you have. You had no right to get yourself into this. Now you must get out—as gracefully as you can, without destroying him."

"But how could I destroy him?"

"A woman can destroy a man, Jemima. I will not have you be that kind of woman!" He turned from the window. "Now you know the consequences of giving your kisses so freely. He took them for more than you intended."

The tears from my eyes spilled down my face onto my hands in my lap.

"Stop that silly crying. It will get you nowhere. I'll help you answer his letter this afternoon if you wish. There are ways of doing what you must do without destroying him. Certainly, you have to put a stop to his romantic notions. But not in one letter. Not all at once. It will take time. You must continue to correspond with him and let him down easily. But you need time for this. Time." He came back across the room and looked down at me. "We all need a little time. Come, now, let's have lessons."

# CHAPTER

## *18*

"When in the course of human events, it becomes necessary for one people to dissolve the political bands which have connected them with another..." Old Sam Tucker, the head of the Provincial Congress, was reading on the courthouse steps. The Declaration of Independence had been rushed in from Philadelphia. It was Monday, the eighth of July. The militia stood lined up below the courthouse steps. Sam Tucker wore a brocaded waistcoat and powdered wig, and his voice rang out clearly.

"A decent respect to the opinions of mankind requires that they should declare the causes which impel them to the separation...."

The crowd could hardly be contained. I was standing next to Betsy Moore. "Does thee see the fat man in the powdered wig? Next to him is thy grandfather."

Indeed, it was. Grandfather Emerson stood out in the crowd, tall and commanding in his frontier clothing. Canoe was with him, listening attentively.

"Oh, Canoe is handsome," Betsy said.

"Hush, Betsy, you're betrothed to my brother."

"And thee is writing to Raymond. Only thee walks in town all the time with John Reid."

"Raymond and I are just corresponding, Betsy. We're only friends."

"I've heard so many stories about Canoe. Is it true he is thy grandfather's son? If so, that would make him thy uncle."

I had never thought of Canoe that way. Sam Tucker went on reading. I should listen. John Reid had excused me from lessons to come and listen. Everyone in town was here, even the Tories. I saw my parents standing off a little to the right of us, with the Moores. Joseph was lined up with the militia. He had joined the week before.

"We hold these truths to be self-evident, that all men are created equal . . ." The words rang out and the crowd began to stomp and cheer. Some of the men threw up their hats. Sam Tucker had to wait for the noise to subside. I looked around, knowing what a wonderful day this was. I should be bursting with pride like everyone else. After all, my father had served with the Provincial Congress on New Jersey's new state constitution that declared our colony's independence from the Crown two whole days before they did it in Philadelphia. My brother Daniel was serving under General Schuyler in the Mohawk Valley, west of Albany, in the heart of the Iroquois Six Nations. And there was Mama, whose essays in the *Pennsylvania Gazette* defended Tom Paine's *Common Sense*, six weeks in a row already.

Why wasn't I feeling the surge of joy that went through the crowd like electricity through Benjamin Franklin's kite?

". . . and by authority of the good people of these colonies, solemnly publish and declare, that these United Colonies are, and of right ought to be, free and independent states; . . ."

The applause was deafening. ". . . that they are absolved from all allegiance to the British Crown. . . ."

"I'll see you later, Betsy," I said.

"Where are thee going?"

"I have something to attend to."

The front door of our house was open, and July sunlight dappled the polished floorboards of the main hall. My shoes echoed, and I made an effort to walk quietly. I went to the end of the hall to my father's study. The house was cool and inviting.

He was in the chair behind Father's desk, half facing the window, which was open. In his hand was a goblet. I stood in the doorway.

He turned, not surprised. "Hello, Jemima."

I curtsied. "Hello, Mr. Reid."

"Why are you back? Everyone is at the reading. I sent you as part of your lessons today, did I not?"

"Yes, sir."

"Well, then? Must I scold on one of the happiest days this young nation has ever had?"

"I hoped you wouldn't. I came back for you. You should be there."

"Wouldn't that look nice? A Tory listening to the reading of the Declaration of Independence. They'd tar and feather me."

"There were other Tories there. Daniel Coxe, Dr. William Bryant from Bloomsbury Court, Isaac Allen and Charles Harrison."

"And do I belong with them?"

"No, sir."

"Where should I have stood, then? With whom? I belong nowhere, Jemima. That's why I am here alone."

"You belong there more than anyone!"

He flung me one of his old dark, forbidding looks, silencing me. I went into the room and sat in a chair near the desk. "You can hear the crowd from here," I said.

"Yes. They won't be contained today."

"Will you come to Mama's celebration dinner tonight?"

"No. Others will be there who don't know of my . . . special circumstances, and for them I'd ruin the celebration. I have my packing to do anyway. I leave at the end of the week."

"I know."

He set the goblet on the desk, twirled the stem around, leaned back in the chair, and contemplated it. The white of his shirt contrasted with his browned face and neck. I sat, intrigued by the sun-bleached hairs on his forearms. I shivered.

"What is it Jemima?"

I shook my head, unable to answer.

He sighed, leaned forward, and rested his arms on his knees. "We're going to have to talk, aren't we?"

I gave him a weak smile. "Yes, sir, I suppose so."

"Lord, don't look at me like that, Jemima." He got up and went to the window. "I've been watching you look at me like that for weeks now, and I haven't known what to do about it."

But he had, for he had managed to be completely in charge of his feelings and continue my lessons with a gentle firmness. It was I who had been so obvious. Several times he'd scolded me when my attention had lapsed. Once, lost under the spell of his voice reading French, I'd accidentally dumped the ink, spilling it onto his breeches. As he'd jumped up, yelling "Damnation," I turned and fled the room in tears, running into Mama in the hallway, who made me turn around and go right back in.

There was a sudden wild cheering in the distance, followed by the firing of muskets. A cannon went off, then church bells.

He smiled at me.

"The bells are from the First Presbyterian," I said. "St. Michael's is closed down."

"I know. Jemima..."

"Reverend Panton is leaving to join the British army. He'll be chaplain of the Prince of Wales Regiment."

"Your mother told me. Jemima..."

"Father will dearly miss playing chess with him."

"Jemima Emerson, will you listen to me!"

There was another burst of cheering in the distance and more musket fire. Then there was silence. "Jemima, I am nine years older than you."

"Eight years and seven months," I said.

"Are you correcting your tutor?" He scowled.

"Yes, sir." I got up and stood in front of him.

"I'm going away to do a filthy, thankless job. I don't know when I'll return."

"But you yourself told me there are lapses in between your missions. You could come back then."

"I have no right to declare my feelings to any woman, with the kind of life I'll be leading."

"Then I shall declare mine to you."

"A properly brought up Christian young woman does not declare her feelings for a man first, Jemima."

"I never was very proper. As my tutor, you should know that, Mr. Reid. But you should also know that I . . . that I have held you in such high esteem since the day you told me I must write to Raymond Moore that I've thought my heart would burst just being around you."

I thought I saw his eyes fill with tears, but he lowered his head. His lashes were very black and thick, and I saw the pulse beating in his temple. He bit his lower lip, and composed himself, and his voice, when he spoke, came from some chamber far inside him that he had kept sealed until now. "These last few weeks, Jemima, I have had to be stern with you so I would not give myself away."

"Well, you've had fair enough practice at it, I would say."

"Oh, Jemima..." His voice broke as he closed his eyes and shook his head. "I have loved you for so long now." He placed his hands just above my hair then lightly touched the top of my head as if I would break. Then, finding out that I was not about to, he slid his hands down my hair to my shoulders and drew me to him. I thought I heard the cannon go off again, but it was the sound of my own heart beating. For his arms were so strong and yet gentle, as I'd dreamed for weeks they would be. And when he kissed me I felt as if the world was exploding inside me for the wonder of it.

When he stopped, I felt an anguish I had not known a body was capable of. And in that moment I possessed and lost the whole world and everything in it and was left with the feeling and the knowledge, which is love, that no matter how we give ourselves we always end up losing. That to love is to lose, the moment we agree to the bargain. And that, being human, we keep standing there wanting to lose more.

He smiled down at me and his eyes welcomed my new-found knowledge with a reassurance that it was all right, after all.

"Do you think you can call me John now?"

He broke my heart when he said that. I couldn't speak. He turned away and reached into the pocket of his linen coat, which was over a nearby chair. "I have something for you."

He drew out a small sack and removed something gold that caught the sunlight.

"Oh, what is it?"

"Something I bought for you when I was in Boston in February."

"In February?"

"I told you I've loved you for a long time." It was a delicate locket of gold and mother-of-pearl.

"Oh, it's beautiful!"

"It's from France." He showed me how it opened, and inside was a likeness of him, deftly sketched. "An artist in Boston did it."

"Oh, John! You've had it all this time!"

"All this time." He smiled. "When I came home from Boston, we fought, if you'll remember. You hadn't done your lessons and I was angry with you."

"You took away my novel. And Bleu. And all the time you had this for me? I hated you then."

"Did you?"

"Well, I did think you looked rather dashing when you came back from Boston. Yet I was angry with you at the same time. And then I got sick and you gave me that book of poems and I was so confused! I didn't know what to think of you."

"Ah, yes, the book of poetry."

"I read it time and time again. It meant so much to me."

"You would have had a hard time convincing me of that. You were still a plague to me."

"Oh, John, don't tease. But tell me, sir, what made you so sure when you were in Boston that I would..."

"That you would learn to love me? I was never sure. But I was hoping." He kissed my forehead. "It was most difficult for me to be stern with you when I loved you so."

"But you managed it just the same."

"Only because I was trying to help you grow up."

"And have I?"

"Yes, Jemima. I would say you have grown up very nicely."

I pinned the locket at the neckline of my short gown, and then I let him kiss me again. Because I had already resolved that if you're afraid of love, your heart will break anyway, only in not half so nice a fashion as it does when you let somebody love you.

# CHAPTER

## *19*

He went away.

He left on a July day when the town was under a stupor of white heat. He packed his saddlebags and took his long musket and put on the hat pinned up with the turkey feather and rode out of town on Star.

One minute he was in Father's study telling me how he expected me to keep on with my lessons, leaving his books for me to read. His hands were on my arms as gentle as goose down, yet like hot irons. He cradled me against his chest, pressed his face against mine, and said my name in terms of endearing promise. The next minute he was striding through the wide hall, and I was standing on our front steps watching him ride down Queen Street.

He left on the pretense that he was gathering information on the war for a Tory paper in New York. He would write for that Tory paper but he would also post notices once a month in the *Pennsylvania Gazette* about his runaway slave, Portia, under the name of Charles Apgar. As long as those notices appeared, I would know he was all right, for his letters to me under his own name might cease at any time.

I stood watching him go, thinking my heart would break. But it didn't. It had to stay whole, for there were too many other things yet to come that would break it.

# CHAPTER
## *20*

"Are you crying again, Jemima Emerson?" I turned from the window in the upstairs hall to see David standing next to me. How tall he'd grown this past summer, how brown he'd gotten, how his voice had deepened.

"All you do is cry over that damned Tory, Reid. Honestly, Jem, I never thought you'd go daft over a Tory."

"Oh, David." I sniffed and turned to put my hands on his shoulders. "Don't scold. You'll be in love one day yourself, and you'll see that politics doesn't have a thing to do with it."

"I should think it would with you. There's Dan, a personal aide to General Schuyler, helping to negotiate with the Iroquois. And Mother getting a whole wagonload of shirts and coats off to the army in New York. And Father with his work in the Congress."

"David . . ." I wiped my eyes and looked up at him coyly. "Don't be angry with me. I can't bear it."

"I'm not angry with you. It's our parents' fault for allowing him to tutor you so long. You couldn't help it. He did sweet-talk you. And everybody knows that girls can't help falling in love when they're sweet-talked. It's all right with me, Jem, if it's what you want."

I hugged him. How dear he was! "I'm so glad Father didn't let you go off with the group of New Jersey militia that left last week."

"Huh! I'm not. They left to join Washington. He needs all the help he can get since Admiral Howe landed all those Redcoats on Staten Island a month ago and General Clinton came up from South Carolina with more. He won't be able to hold New York."

"But we can't let you go yet. You're not even sixteen."

"Some of our boys were fourteen and fifteen when they fought at Lexington and Concord."

"Time enough for that, David. Like Lucy says, time enough for drums."

"All of a sudden Lucy is the philosopher in the household. And people worry about slavery. Lucy's long since forgotten that she's owned. She practically runs everybody around here. Jem, have you heard that Grandfather Emerson and Canoe are leaving?"

"No. Where are they going?"

"They've gotten news that a Cherokee war party attacked the whole white frontier, from southern Virginia to northern Georgia. They're off to try to make peace with the Indians at the request of the Continental Congress. Damn, I wish I could go with them!"

"Oh, David, everyone's going away!"

"Now, don't you start that crying again. And you'd better get to the shop. Father's looking for you."

Canoe and Grandfather came into the shop later that hot August morning to pick up a bundle of supplies. I helped Father wrap the coffee and cakes of chocolate, spices, sugar cones, and linen thread. Canoe stood before me at the counter.

"John Reid will be fine," he said.

I looked at him. His eyes held warm sympathy and were understanding, but more than that they held a knowledge. Was it possible he knew of Reid's activities? Grandfather and Canoe certainly belonged to the network of Patriots in Trenton. Had John confided in them, maybe even used their advice for his travels?

"Gathering information for a Tory paper can be dangerous, Canoe," I said.

"Gathering information for any reason in wartime is dangerous," he said, "but Reid is a smart man." He set a small sack down on the counter. I knew it was pemmican, Canoe's way of comforting me. "Thank you, Canoe."

He met my eyes. "He thinks much of you, Mr. Reid."

"And I think much of him."

"He came to see us before he left. Your grandfather helped him map out his route."

So it was true. They did know of his activities. Still, it was not to be spoken of outright. Canoe nodded, took his bundle, and padded out into the August heat.

In late August a letter came:

> I am very fine here in New York but I am thwarted in my work for the time being. I must first make friends with the right people who can help me. So far it is all social discourse and I am not allowed to proceed further until I establish myself. I know my articles are needed for the paper and it pains me to sit and sip tea and rejoice in General Howe's attack on New York, successful though it was,

when I could be reporting the events. I hope all
is well with you.

Your obedient servant,
John Reid

I knew what he was about. He was in New York making
friends with Tories, ingratiating himself by sipping tea. It
must be killing him. I destroyed the letter immediately as
he had instructed.

"Read Daniel's letter to me again, Betsy."

"Oh, Jem, I've read it to thee two times. Anyway, it's
private, I've told thee that."

"I don't want those pages. Just read the other parts so I
can remember to tell Mama when I get home. She hasn't
heard from him."

"Thee would be wise not to tell thy mother anything."
But she dug the letter out of her basket.

> . . . we did our best to evacuate the supplies stored
> here at Fort Lee after the fall of Fort Washington.
> But wagons were impossible to find. General
> Greene, my commander, managed to get the am-
> munition away, then sent five hundred of us out
> to guard the places where the British might land.
> But somehow, in the night, they climbed a place
> in the Palisades we never thought they could ma-
> neuver. They captured over two thousand of our
> men at Fort Washington. When we discovered they
> had climbed the Palisades, they were only eight
> miles away. So we officers gave the order to flee,
> leaving our tents and cannon. Thousands of us
> marched off, leaving our breakfasts on the cooking
> fires.

Your brother is with me. I was dispatched on my new assignment in August and told to join Washington because my superiors perceived me to be a capable officer with somewhat of a reputation for both gallantry and common sense. I asked to have Raymond accompany me. He has proved his worth. On the long journey down from the north I was plagued with a persistent cough and a cold in my chest and he took good care of me. But it's November now and my men are quite ragged. My own coat has become shabby, but I worry that with all the marching my men's shoes will soon be gone. At least I still ride dear old faithful Gulliver, who fares well. I shall not give further description beyond saying that this was an unhappy day for our Cause.

I shivered as the cold December wind whistled down Queen Street. "I hate the British, Betsy."

"Thee mustn't hate."

"I'll hate all I want to. And if I see one Redcoat in this town, I'll kill him."

"Thee couldn't kill a fly."

"I could. Dan taught me how to shoot a musket. I hate them with their fine, fancy warships and their good uniforms. I hate this town too. Every day someone else leaves. Reverend Spencer left, and now the Presbyterians don't have a minister either."

"My father says Reverend Spencer has a hundred guineas on his head for his Patriotic activities. Thee would flee too. But thee does not need ministers to pray."

Just then I caught sight of a broadside nailed to a post of the Black Horse Tavern. "Look, Betsy, it's one of General

Howe's announcements about his protection papers!" We went closer to read.

"'We hereby do declare and make known,'" Betsy read, "'to all men that every person who, within sixty days from the date hereof, shall appear and claim the benefit of this proclamation and at the same time testify his obedience to the laws by subscribing a declaration of the words therein is promised a free and general pardon.'"

Below it, in script on heavy parchment, was a copy of the pardon issued by General William Howe when he entered New Jersey.

"I think it's the ugliest thing I've ever seen," I said.

"Has thy father signed one, Jem?"

"My father would never. What about yours?"

"Quakers do not take oaths. Did thee not hear how Stacy Potts refused to take the oath to the Patriotic Cause, even though he's a true Patriot?"

Again we viewed the broadside. "Let's tear it down, Betsy," I said.

"Thee wouldn't dare. Why, it's the King's own! General Howe acts for the King!"

"All the more reason!" And without further ado I took a step onto the wooden walk and grasped the bottom of the broadside. It came loose and I stood looking at it, larger than life in my hands.

"Hide it under thy cloak, quickly," Betsy said. I did so. We looked up and down Queen Street, but it was empty. We hurried in the direction of my house, where we were going to do some sewing for the army.

Ripping down the broadside had given me great satisfaction. For the past week, I had been so worried and distracted that I thought I would lose my wits and my senses altogether. I'd received another letter from John in late September. Also, the first notice in the *Gazette* about the missing slave, Portia, had appeared, just in case the letter hadn't gotten to me. The letter had been fine enough although convoluted. I managed to decipher that John was doing what he wanted to do and making progress. Then in late November, just about a week ago, another letter came.

This one told about the hanging in late September of Nathan Hale, who had been spying for the Americans. "His mission was planned badly," John wrote. "His face was marked by exploding powder, so he was easily recognizable, and he had a cousin serving with the British. We are now hearing that the American intelligence service is better organized, so we have to be wary of them."

Still, I'd been worried. And then came the letter from Dan about the fall of Fort Washington. The Cause was faring poorly.

"Ah, Jem, we were just speaking of you. Major Barnes has a complaint against you. Come and defend yourself."

My father looked over his spectacles as I entered his shop to relieve him for his noonday meal. The man at the counter was smartly dressed, and I recognized him as our neighbor on Queen Street, Mr. Barnes.

He bowed to me cordially. He'd been the high sheriff of Hunterdon County, but in mid-July the Provincial Congress had brought charges against him as a Tory and he'd resigned. It was probably he who'd put up the broadside. And now he was in my father's shop in all his fine clothes calling himself Major. Whatever for, I couldn't imagine.

"Jem, Mr. Barnes is now a major of the First Battalion, New Jersey Volunteers. He'll be leaving soon to serve with the British army."

A British officer. What could I say?

"Major Barnes claims he was standing on his verandah this morning and saw you tear down the broadside posted on the Black Horse Tavern."

"It was no ordinary broadside, Jemima," Barnes said. "It was a proclamation from General Howe."

"I know what it was."

"Then you did tear it down?"

"Yes, sir."

"Why, Jemima?" my father asked.

"Because I'd just seen a letter that Betsy Moore received from Dan that tells how the army had to flee Fort Lee and how the men's shoes are practically gone and Dan's coat is so shabby. That's why."

My father took off his spectacles and wiped them.

"Ah yes," Barnes said. "Well, I quite understand your childish impulsiveness, then."

"It wasn't childish impulsiveness. I'm not a child. I knew what I was doing." I looked at his fine clothes as I said it.

"Impulsiveness," he insisted, "that can only bring trouble to your family when the British arrive."

"Oh, and are they arriving, Major Barnes?"

"Jemima," Father warned.

"As far as trouble goes, my family already has trouble. We don't know where Dan is or that he isn't cold and starving."

"I understand, young lady," he said, "but your brother is suffering the fortunes of war."

"So did General Howe's broadside."

He sighed. "It's a pity that nice Loyalist tutor you had left town. You're a feisty one, Jemima Emerson. It seems he was the only person who could ever keep you in line. Take my word for it—when the British reach Trenton, such foolish actions will bring dire results." He turned to

Father. "James, I implore you as an old friend and neighbor to sign the loyalty oath. When it's a question of being shot as a traitor or imprisoned or losing all your worldly goods, prudence should take the place of valor."

"Thank you for your concern, John."

"But you won't, of course, will you?"

"A loyalty oath to the King? John, I don't know if my son is alive or dead right now. If we had a flag to symbolize what we're fighting for here in these colonies, I tell you I'd be tempted to fly it when the British reach Trenton. But we don't have one."

"Then when they come here, take your family out of town, James. Leave, like the others."

"I have my home and my shop," Father said simply.

Major Barnes drew his cloak around him. "I see there's no influencing you. At least send your family out of town, then. Think on it." He took my father's hand in both his own, scowled at me, and left.

"Father, I'm so proud of you."

He was tidying up the counter. "What he said was true, Jem, every word of it. And I'm not happy with you for what you did today, either."

"I did what I thought was right."

"I never have been able to control you, Jemima. As Major Barnes said, John Reid was the only one who ever could."

"You're the one who is always telling us to have convictions."

"There's a difference between convictions and foolishness."

"And I suppose you're not being foolish refusing to sign the loyalty oath?"

"Don't be saucy with me, miss. I won't have it. In light of what you did today, I'm thinking seriously of sending you and your mother to Otter Hall if the British come."

"And you?"

"You heard me. I have my shop."

"Well, I won't go. And Mother won't, either."

"Never mind about your mother. You'll go if I say."

"I shan't!"

"Jemima Emerson, you're wanting a birching, talking to me like that. And even though I never have, I will if you defy me in this matter."

"I don't care if you do! I won't go! I won't leave you!" I burst out crying.

He didn't know what to do. He looked startled and confused. He came from behind the counter with a look so stricken, I knew I would never forget it. I ran to him and he held me in his arms. "Hush, hush, child."

"Father, don't make me go to Otter Hall. The family is all separated as it is, and I don't want to leave you alone."

He quieted me, then promised he would not make me go. He promised we would stay together always. "The British can't separate us," he said. "Why, the British probably won't even come to Trenton. We're getting upset over nothing."

Five days later the British did come to Trenton. But the retreating American army, Daniel with them, came first.

# CHAPTER

## 21

We were at supper that night, with the December wind beating in dark waves against the windows, when the front door burst open, admitting a gust of cold air.

"The American army is nearing Princeton!"

It was David. He came in with a clatter, his musket slung over his shoulder. He set it down in the hall and stood with the rain dripping from the cape of his rifle frock.

"Is that any reason to interrupt a man's supper?" My father looked up from his soup.

"No, sir."

"You're late."

"I know. I stopped to talk about the news."

"I can't imagine with whom. Except for Quakers, there's hardly anybody left in town."

"With Stacy Potts. Washington's army left Brunswick with three thousand men and should reach Princeton tomorrow."

Mother uttered a small cry and put her napkin to her mouth. Father cast her a worried look and spoke even more sternly to David.

"How many times have I told you not to worry your mother? Take off your coat and stop dripping on the floor. I'd still like to maintain some civility in this house, and the approach of an army is no reason to act otherwise."

"I should be with the army," David said, sitting down.

"You push me too far, young man," Father warned. It was an ongoing argument between David and Father. Our militia had left, and Father had managed to keep David from signing on. He was still only fifteen.

"Enlistments expired yesterday, the last day of November," David said. "Washington needs men. I'm joining up when he comes through. You've got to let me, Father."

My father knew he could not hold David back any longer. "There will be no joining up until your father gives permission, David," Mother said. "Come, now, eat your soup."

David obeyed. My father studied him. "Who gave you the news?"

"I told you. Stacy Potts."

"Where did he get it from?"

"A spy."

Now it was I who uttered a small cry in my throat. My father looked at me and shook his head. "A spy, is it? I'd heard Washington was improving his spying network. But your spy could just as well have been British, David, passing along the wrong information."

"The army's retreating," David insisted.

"Oh, now, that's news, isn't it?" my father said sarcastically. "They've *been* retreating for months. Since they lost the battle of Long Island in August, it's been retreat, retreat, retreat. White Plains, Fort Washington, Fort Lee, all lost. Washington's been retreating across the Jerseys since November. Are they still an army? That's what I want to know."

"Yes," David said, "from what I've heard."

"Well, that is news. Eat your supper now and no more talk. We're upsetting your mother."

"I'm all right, James," Mama said. "I'm fine. Do you think Dan is with them?"

"Most likely."

"How far behind are the British?" she asked David.

"Not far behind, Mother. Cornwallis entered New Brunswick as Washington left. They cannonaded each other across the Raritan River."

"James, do you suppose all those rumors we've heard about the British looting and destroying and killing livestock are true?" she asked Father.

"It is wartime, Sarah," he said simply.

"Then we should take our valuables to Otter Hall."

"I should like you and Jemima to go to Otter Hall as well," Father said.

"We'll stay together as a family, James," Mother said firmly. "Most people have left town, but there are still some good people here."

How I admired Mother's courage. All through November, when the news went from bad to worse and I knew how worried she was about Dan, she kept on with her sewing for the army and her letters. Her essays appeared in just about every issue of the *Pennsylvania Gazette* these days. The last one I'd read had said that Washington was paying for the needs of his army out of his own pocket and that our men were tying pieces of cloth around their legs and rags around their feet. Hundreds of them were so sick they could barely walk. And the doctors had no medicines, no spirits, no oils.

I didn't know where Mother got her information. She had been responsible for getting two wagonloads of clothes north to the army in November. Perhaps the driver whom she had paid to take them had brought back news.

"James, how many pairs of shoes do we have in the shop?" she asked.

"I don't know that we have any." He met her eyes across the table.

"But you have blankets. And I'm sure you could get other warm clothing from Otter Hall."

"Of course, my dear. I should have thought of it."

"As soon as we've finished supper, I'd like the key to the shop," she said. "Lucy and I will see what is there. Jemima, eat, child. You look so pale. Don't let the approaching British army frighten you. I was in Boston when it was occupied, and I assure you, the British are not savages."

Gingerly, after Mama had left the table, Cornelius came into the room. "Sir, if I could talk with you."

"Yes, Cornelius," Father said. "If you have any suggestions, I'd be pleased to hear them. Sit. This is no time for formality."

Cornelius took a chair a bit away from the table. "Sir, if the British come, they'll take me. They'll promise me all kinds of things."

"They'll promise you freedom," my father said.

"Yes, sir, that they will."

"But they won't give it." My father was puffing on his pipe. "What do you have in mind?"

"Just that it wouldn't be good for me to be here when they come. David neither, he bein' almost of fightin' age. I could take him and join up with the army when it comes through."

My father contemplated this. David immediately dropped his fork and was staring, open-mouthed.

"You can't fire a musket, Cornelius," my father said.

"I could learn."

"I know you could. David here could teach you within the next day or so. Couldn't you, David?"

"Oh yes, sir! I think Cornelius's idea is a good one. I don't think he or I should stay. John Fitch has gone across the river to Bucks County."

"If I were John Fitch I would go to Bucks County too," Father said, "with the large contracts he has for the repairing of American arms."

"I would look out for David, sir," Cornelius said. "And him bein' with me, you'd be sure I'd come back."

Father set down his pipe. Then he looked around the table, to each of us in turn. "Jemima, go into my study and get some parchment, a pen, and some ink, and bring it here."

I stood up.

"Cornelius, it's time," my father said. "I shall write up the documents tonight and set you and Lucy free. David, go and get Stacy Potts and ask him to come and witness the documents. I shall register them with the courthouse tomorrow."

And so that evening my father drew up the papers and gave Lucy and Cornelius their freedom. We all sat around the dining room table and watched. Stacy Potts arrived and approved, being a Quaker. "Although I do wish you had done it in the Lord's good sunlight, James, so I wouldn't have to get drenched in the rain."

"Lucy"—my father looked at her over his spectacles—"I was hoping you'd stay on with us for the proper recompense. There will be some hard days ahead."

She stood there with her hands on her hips. "Now, Mr. Emerson, where would I go?"

"She'll be stayin'." Cornelius stood with his arm around

her shoulder. "And I'll be back someday too, if you need me."

"We need you, Cornelius, that we do." Father answered, choked with emotion. "You just keep an eye on David for us."

"You mean I can go? I can join when the army comes through?" David couldn't believe it.

I saw Father seek Mother's eyes across the table. "It's best, Sarah," he said. "Cornelius is right. He'll be in more danger here when the British come through."

"Of course, James." Mother stood up. "Come here, David."

He went to her and she looked up at him. "If you insist on being a soldier in Washington's army, you must be a good soldier. Remember all we've taught you and always say your prayers."

"I will, Mama," David said.

"What is it, Jem?"

I lingered in the dining room when everyone had left. "Father, do you think the spy was John?"

"No, I think it was idle gossip. Such news is not new. You've heard from him, haven't you?"

"The last I heard he was inside British lines in New York. He said there might not be letters for a while."

"He'll be all right, Jem. His work is needed more now than ever. Go to bed. Tomorrow you must take Bleu to Otter Hall."

When I awoke the next morning Father and David and Cornelius had already taken a load of furnishings to Otter Hall. Mama's good silver pieces and her best pewter and Delft plates went. So did the Persian carpet and Mama's wedding chest, which was filled with two crewel bedcovers and some of Father's precious books.

When they came back around noon on that second day of December, they said that General Washington had arrived in town.

"Where?" I asked excitedly.

"He's been seen down at the river," Father said. "He seems to have about half his force with him. We inquired and were told that Dan and his men are still at Princeton."

"Where do you think he'll stay when he's in town?" I asked. "Oh, I would so love to see him!"

Father smiled at me indulgently. "His men have been destroying bridges and gathering boats all up and down the river. It looks as if they plan to build a makeshift embarkation dock. I think they mean to cross into Pennsylvania."

"In this weather, the way the river is so swollen from rain?" Mother asked.

"It's better than standing and fighting the British, the condition they're in," David said.

"But doesn't Washington have to stay somewhere?" I persisted.

"He'll most likely be anywhere on the roads between here and Princeton," Father speculated. "Probably staying at random houses along the way. And the less anybody knows about where he is, the better. God help the man. The fate of the country is with him, and it doesn't look like a very good fate right now."

I fell silent. Father put his hand on my shoulder. "He's retreating, Jem. When a man retreats, he doesn't send out invitations to tea. Here, where are you off to, David?"

He was on his way out the door, musket in hand. "You said Cornelius and I could go down and enlist this afternoon."

"You'll sit down and eat a proper meal first," Father

ordered. "Washington has enough hungry men. He doesn't need more."

That afternoon I made a trip to Otter Hall with Lucy and my father. I dressed in my warmest clothes and followed the wagon on Bleu. It was a sad ride. Bleu's and my happy times were over now. I patted him to warm my hands and tried to keep from crying.

The December wind whistled around me. I pulled my blanket coat tighter. My eyes darted up and down the deserted streets. Perhaps Washington would just take a ride through town and then I could get a glimpse of him in his fine blue coat with the buff facings and his sword and polished boots. Dan had written about what a commanding figure he was and how the men were so in awe of him.

Everything would be all right in my threadbare soul, I thought, if I could just see him. But I did not.

# CHAPTER

## 22

It was dusk on the seventh of December. At midmorning we'd had word that the rest of the army had arrived. Mother and Father and Lucy and I bundled up some clothes, warm blankets, and food, and headed for the river. Along the way we picked up the Moores.

The scene when we arrived around one in the afternoon was like a nightmare. The river was full of rowboats, ferry boats, and galleys from the Pennsylvania navy. It was a day of gray skies and no sun and biting cold, which added to the nightmarish quality. The crossings from New Jersey to Pennsylvania had begun in early afternoon, and I was desperately afraid Dan would cross before I found him.

Betsy Moore and I had gotten permission from our parents to wander up and down the banks and try to find Dan. We'd been searching for what seemed like hours, meeting each other every so often to commiserate and start looking again. It was getting to be dusk already. All up and down the river where the endless stream of the army was gathered, bonfires and torches were lit, adding an unreal quality to an already unreal scene.

I turned suddenly, bumping into a tall officer who was shouting orders at the stunned and weakened men as they approached the embarkation point.

"Damnation!" He turned to peer down at me. "What's this? You shouldn't be about alone in this mess, miss."

"My parents are nearby. I'm Jemima Emerson from Trenton, sir. I'm looking for my brother, Daniel. He's a captain. He wears the blue and red of the Second New Jersey."

"Our men wear anything they can get their hands on these days, miss." His uniform was filthy and ragged, but he still wore his crimson silken sash and sword, and in spite of a day's worth of beard he bowed politely.

"Lieutenant Colonel David Henley, at your service. From Trenton, you say? I didn't think there was anyone left in Trenton who cared. I did see some New Jersey men over there to the left, near the artillery." He gestured beyond the rim of torchlight. "This way, soldier, right here, come on, lad," he was saying.

They came up to him like ghosts out of the dusk and wordlessly boarded the boats. They were like skeletons, scarecrows. Their clothes hung in tatters. The once-fine coats of the Continental army were muddied and torn. Rags were wrapped around their necks, and their breeches were threadbare, with bloodied legs showing through. The lucky ones had tied blankets around them with pieces of rope. Their knapsacks and cartridge boxes and muskets and canteens dangled from their emaciated bodies.

Some had sores on their faces, and their lips were cracked and blue from the cold. Only a few had shoes. Most had rags wrapped around their feet, and their hair hung limp and unkempt. Many stumbled, held up by comrades.

But they kept coming, passing me with eyes that saw nothing because they had seen too much. And yet their eyes had a peculiar fire in them, a dull, persistent gaze. I could not take my eyes from them as they streamed by me. They looked like a lost tribe that had wandered the earth homeless. Yet something about them, some sense of shared experience, made them look as if they all belonged together. That look made them an army and clothed them far better in sameness than any bright uniform with dashing swords and plumes and buttons.

I found Dan standing near some artillery pieces with a group of tattered soldiers. The torchlight behind him silhouetted his figure against the bleak winter sky.

I would have known him anywhere. I would have known him in hell. He said something to one of his men. His broad shoulders were straight and commanding in the faded blue and red coat. His breeches were dirty, his boots worn and muddy. His wrists were thin and chafed. But he wore his sword with authority, and there was something about the way he held his head and wore his cocked hat that would make me single him out in a field of a hundred men.

"Daniel!" I could barely speak his name, lest the speaking of it make him disappear. And I could barely see him for my tears.

He turned. "Jem? Is it really you?"

I ran to him, slipping on the frozen ground.

"Be careful, Jem. Don't fall." His voice was older, huskier, more confident. Oh, how could he be confident in the middle of all this?

I ran across the frozen ground into his arms.

Both of my brothers crossed the river within the next hour. There was scarcely time for Dan and Betsy to have a few moments together and for him to visit with Mother and Father.

Scarcely time for him to tell the Moores that he'd had to leave Raymond north of New Brunswick at the house of a farmer and his wife, for Raymond had fallen ill with dysentery and fever. He gave the Moores the name of the farmer and told them where he lived.

Mother and Lucy gave him the bread and meat they had brought, and he shared it with his men, along with the blankets and blanket coats. Father's voice was low and sad when he told Dan that there hadn't been any shoes in his shop to bring. I know he considered it a personal failure.

The crossings continued far into the night and the afternoon of the next day while we stayed in our house. Father closed his shop, the first time I ever remember him doing so.

"What good is a shop," he said, "when I couldn't supply my son and his men with what they needed?"

At supper that night there was a knock on the door. Father went to answer it and came back to the dining room with Stacy Potts.

"Did thee not hear the music?" Mr. Potts asked.

"No," Mother answered, "we have been in the house all day."

"Oh yes," he said, "the British and Hessians came into town with much music and display. They came shortly after the last of the Americans crossed the river a few hours ago."

Hessians! Paid soldiers from Germany hired by George the Third! I drew in my breath. Lucy had told me stories about the Hessians. She said that Hessian grenadiers had killed more American soldiers than any other Hessian unit on American soil!

"Would you sit and sup with us, Mr. Potts?" Mother asked calmly.

"Thank thee, no, ma'am. It has been a tiring day." He

smiled and winked at my father. "The Americans, James, met them with a shower of grapeshot from across the river."

My father nodded in solemn approval.

"But I will not keep thee from thy supper." He hesitated. Then, "James, these will be difficult days for us all when the town is occupied."

"I've given it much thought, Stacy."

"I know my Patriotism has been in question since I refused to take the oath to the Cause."

"I know your Quaker faith forbids oaths, Stacy. We have no doubts as to your Patriotism."

"Thee is kind. I would hope thee has no doubts in the days to come."

"And why should I, Stacy?"

"My house has already been inspected as a possible headquarters for the Hessian commander, Johann Gottlieb Rall. If he chooses to occupy it, I will be an impartial and gracious host."

"There is nothing else you can do, Stacy."

He nodded, bowed to my mother, and went with my father to the door. When my father came back he looked at us. "Stacy Potts is one of the most prosperous and decent men in town. His house is probably the most commodious. I know him to be a true friend and Patriot. I'll hear nothing in the way of disparaging remarks about him if they occupy his house."

"We'll include him in our evening prayers, James," Mother said.

# CHAPTER

## 23

Colonel Johann Rall rode into town on the twelfth with his five hundred grenadiers. They had fierce mustaches and arrived marching to a brass band. From our windows I could see Hessians in the street, going in and out of the houses on Queen, houses that had belonged to our friends. It made me angry seeing these black-uniformed men in our town. Father, who went to his shop that morning, said they called themselves Knyphausen and that they were in the village school and Presbyterian church. He told me I was not to go out of the house.

I did not see why I should be a prisoner in my own town. So when he went back to the shop after his noon meal and Mama and Lucy were busy, I slipped out. No one bothered me as I ventured forth, and so I went on and before I knew it I was strolling through most of the town. When I got back, it was almost suppertime and Father met me in the hall. "Where have you been?"

"I just went for a little walk, Father."

"Didn't I tell you not to go out?" He looked so fierce, his face was flushed. His hair nearly stood on end.

"But this is our town. We can't let—"

Before I had finished he was grasping my shoulders with both hands, shaking me roughly. "If you go outside this house again without permission, I'll take a birch rod to you! I've half a mind to do it now! When will you learn to obey?"

I saw more fear than anger in his eyes. "I'm sorry, Father," I said. "I won't do it again." Mother and Lucy hovered behind him.

"I never was strict enough with you, Jemima Emerson," he said, "and now I rue the day!" He released me. I ran to Mama, who put her arm around me. "She'll obey you, James. Won't you, Jem?"

I nodded, but he strode in to supper without looking at me. At the table he said that people who came into the shop had told him the Jaegers, who wore green uniforms trimmed with red, were at the old French and Indian War barracks down near the river. He would go to his shop every day, he said, for if he didn't, they might ransack it. He had heard that the Knyphausen regiment was using the parsonage of Dr. Elihu Spencer and ripping into his book collection to light fires and clean their boots.

The next morning Father came in from milking Silly, our cow, whom Mother had originally named Priscilla. "Jemima, you've not fed the chickens yet."

"I thought I'd do it after breakfast, Father."

"Do it now. It's a simple enough task, yet you can't seem to remember to do it. Well, go on."

It had been my job since David and Cornelius had left. I couldn't see the fuss over a few straggly chickens. Yet he was determined not to let up on me, it seemed. "But Father—"

"Are you about to give me an argument?"

"No, sir."

"Then go!"

I put on my blanket-coat and went out into the cold. I thought his anger was all out of proportion. Then I thought it was probably the news he'd received yesterday, that the Hessians had two brass three-pounder guns in the church-yard of St. Michael's. I hated going into the barn without Bleu there and I sorely missed Chauncy the goat, who used to nibble at my petticoat in greeting. I squinted my eyes in the dimness. There were Romeo and Juliet, Father's faithful carriage horses, and old Silly, all munching their breakfasts.

I was just about inside the door when I felt someone grab my wrist. I cried out, but a hand was clapped over my mouth. I thrashed my free arm around, but then both my wrists were secured behind my back.

Fear knifed through me. I kicked, but he was too strong for me. A Hessian! I screamed, but the sound died in my throat. I kicked again.

"Ow! You little devil! You haven't changed a bit, have you?" He laughed his old familiar laugh, and a surge of relief went through me. John!

But I couldn't say his name. His hand was still over my mouth, and with the other still gripping my wrists behind me he led me into the shadows. "Ssh. You must promise to speak in whispers before I release you."

I nodded agreeably and he let me go. "John, what are you—"

"Shush. Must I shush you?" And he did then, by drawing me to him and kissing me. I shushed very nicely then for a few minutes, struck dumb by the wonder of his kisses, the look in his eyes, the wonder of *him*, standing there whole and alive. Tears came as I reached up to touch his dear face. He looked drawn, tired, and lean. He had grown a beard, too.

"John, what are you doing here?"

"I've come to see you," he teased maddeningly.

"You *know* what I mean!"

"I'm working."

"Do be serious."

"But I am. See?" And he motioned to a bundle at his feet. "I have my paper and supplies. I'm still writing for the Tory newspaper. And I peddle a little tobacco on the side. It's an easy way to get into an enemy camp. The Hessians are always eager for a smoke. I have a letter of introduction and safe passage from the British authorities, along with a copy of my loyalty oath to the King. The American army has a price on my head."

"John!"

He smiled. "It's to complete my disguise. I've built a reputation as a fine writer for Tory newspapers. And I sell nothing but the best tobacco. Your father has promised to be out of it for the next day or so in his shop."

"Father knows you are here?"

"Weren't you told to come out and feed the chickens?" He smiled more widely now, flashing his fine white teeth. Oh Lord, how I'd missed him! "He was provoked when you hadn't done so yet. I see they still need me to keep you in line."

"Will you be serious?"

"All right. When he came out to milk Silly and found me, he went right back inside and got some fresh-baked bread and cured ham. While I ate, he told me what he knows of the troops in town."

"You're working for Washington."

He made a deep bow. "He needed someone with a Tory reputation who knew the town. The Tories here would point out a stranger. But I'm well known. I left loyal to the Crown and I've come back the same way. Now you must recite some lessons for me."

I gaped. "At a time like this?"

"Yes." And he took my hands and led me to sit on a bale of hay. "Your father says you might add to what he told me. I understand you slipped out of the house against his wishes yesterday afternoon and took a nice long walk." He was scowling, the way he used to do when I'd been naughty.

"Yes," I admitted.

"My ever-disobedient little pupil. This one time I'm grateful, but you mustn't disobey your father again. Suppose I had been a Hessian grabbing you just now? Do you know what would have happened to you?"

I blushed but did not answer.

"Well? Do you?" he insisted.

"Yes, John. I won't do it again. I promise."

"Good. Now, can you tell me what you saw on that nice long walk? Are there any British in town?"

"Twenty of them at the Friends Meeting House on Third Street."

"Good. Excellent. Any others?"

"No. Everyone else is Hessian. They're horrible-looking, John."

"Yes, they are. Where is the artillery? Can you remember?"

I thought for a moment. "At the Methodist church. And our own English church. The Hessians hold over a dozen buildings below the Assunpink Creek, and they're even out on the Penny Town Road. I couldn't help noticing things."

"I'm glad you did. You always had a sharp mind, Jem.

But don't let your curiosity or your sauciness get you into trouble. You're in an occupied town now. You must be careful and mind your parents. One more thing. Have you noticed any of the enemy building boats?"

I shook my head firmly. "No, but yesterday Colonel Rall had a parade. He ordered the cannon to be drawn forth and his musicians played the French horns and trumpets and drums, and all his officers made a grand entrance. They say he's quite mad over music and pomp. But oh, how I long for the sound of our fifes and drums."

He kissed my forehead tenderly. "You'll hear them soon again, I promise."

"John, David, and Cornelius have joined with Washington. And Raymond Moore is very ill and close to dying. Dan had to leave him north of New Brunswick."

"Now aren't you glad you wrote to him as long as you could?"

"Yes. If I could get a letter through, I'd write now. Would you mind terribly?"

"I would mind if you didn't. Now listen to me. You are not to tell your mother or Lucy that I'm here. I'll be in town today, then back across the river."

"And will you be back?"

"I don't know. I do as I'm told, as should you. I'm not the only agent working for Washington. Are you doing your reading?"

"Oh, John!" I giggled. He took my chin between his thumb and forefinger. "You have done very well with your lessons today."

Tears came to my eyes. He held me close. "Go inside now before your mother gets concerned. Or your father wonders why I've kept you for so long. I'll continue to place ads in the *Gazette* so you'll know I'm still alive."

# CHAPTER

## 24

Saturday, the fourteenth, Sunday, and Monday were very quiet. Then on Tuesday the British sent a patrol out to Penny Town, north of Trenton. They were fired upon and one soldier was wounded. Father said it was General Philemon Dickinson's militia who fired, Americans who lived in the area. They struck the British at random and disappeared again into the woods.

That same day the Pennsylvania militia landed thirty men at the ferry picket post Rall had set up south of town. They harassed the Hessians with gunfire and withdrew across the river.

"At least Washington isn't just sitting there across the river," Father said. He was elated.

Wednesday morning we were awakened by cannon fire at dawn. It echoed in the distance, carried on the brittle morning air. That evening Father came in from the shop to tell us a landing party of fifty men had attacked the Jaegers at the ferry picket post and withdrawn to the other side of the river.

Thursday morning dawned bright and clear. Father was

in a cheery mood. "Would you like to come with me to see the Moores today, Jem? I think we should pay a visit to our neighbors and see how they're faring."

Father and I had a nice visit at the Moores', but I came home sneezing and with a raspy throat. Mother fussed over me and declared I was feverish. Father said I should have a bowl of Lucy's soup and go right to bed. I protested, but he scowled sternly.

"I want to sup with your mama alone," he said. "I have much to talk about."

I heard him telling her that the Moores wanted to travel to find Raymond but could not leave their farm. But I thought there was some other matter pressing him, for I'd seen him and Mr. Moore huddled together before we left.

"I'm glad thee responded to my word to come," Mr. Moore had said, "and I'm glad I could act as intermediary."

Something sinister was going on, I was sure of it. Lucy fed me and gave me one of Mama's concoctions for fever, although I had been in a state of fever since John Reid had shown up. But I couldn't tell her that.

No sooner was I in my flannel nightdress than I heard my parents arguing. I waited until Lucy left the room, then slipped into the hall.

"James, on such a bitter night. It terrifies me."

"It isn't like you to know fear, Sarah."

"It isn't like me to show it. I show it now because I saw the orders issued by General Howe threatening to hang without trial anyone firing upon or molesting British soldiers or peaceable inhabitants."

"I have no intention of firing upon anyone. I'm simply delivering dry foodstuffs and rum to General Dickinson's militia in the woods of Penny Town. I'm a merchant doing business."

"Why didn't the note come directly to you? Why to the Moores?"

"Sarah, be sensible. It was the only way they could get the note to me. Isaac Moore sent word to the shop yesterday that I should come out. Those men are freezing in the woods, and if I can help them I will."

"On such a night you can be tracked easily in the snow. You'll endanger them."

"I'm only taking a horse. The snow will cover our tracks easily. I know the roads better than the Hessians. You must allow me this, Sarah. It's something I can do to help. How do you think I've felt seeing my town taken over and being able to do nothing?"

I didn't hear Mother's reply, but I heard him telling her to secure the doors. "I'll go out the back way and stay overnight with the militia. Don't wait up for me."

After he left, I went to the window in the upstairs hall and saw him come out of the barn with Romeo. He threw a bag of supplies over the horse's back. He wore his civilian clothes, for he had no uniform, yet I was thrilled with the importance of his mission. He had only his musket. I watched him pull the hood of his blanket-coat up over his head and ride off into the flurries of snow.

I slept the sleep of the dead that night from the fever concoction Lucy had given me. I awoke to see the sun slanting across the floor in my room the way it did when it was very late. For a moment I could not figure out what was going on.

I had been sound asleep one moment, but a sound had pulled me awake the next. There it was again.

A scream. It pierced the air, long and protracted and filled with agony. I recognized it instantly as Mother's, and it pulled me out of my childhood forever and thrust me headlong into the world of adulthood, a world where nothing was ever secure again.

I did not have to ask what was wrong went I went downstairs and found Lucy and Mother in the parlor. I knew, from the look in Mama's eyes, that Father was dead.

# CHAPTER

## 25

"Child, you gotta eat sumpthin'."

"Lucy, if I'd gotten up on time it wouldn't have happened."

"That ain't true. Your papa weren't killed here. He be killed someplace on his mission last night. They just leave him in the shop. What could you have done?"

"I could have gone with him. I know how to shoot. Dan taught me. I could have killed them."

"Hush. 'Nuf talk about killin' now."

"Why did they do it, Lucy? They had no reason."

"They don't need no reason."

"That's no good, Lucy. It doesn't make sense."

"It's all we got, child. These times got no sense."

"They beat him to death. They smashed his head in."

"Hush. Don't say it."

"I have to say it. I hurt inside, Lucy. It helps the hurting."

"Then say it."

"They beat him to death. They smashed his head in. And they ransacked his shop. He's dead. My father is dead."

"Yes, he's dead. I saw him."

"I saw him too, Lucy. The Indian women from Otter Hall let me see him."

"They shouldn't have."

"I wanted to. I had to. His eyes were open. How can you be dead with your eyes open, Lucy?"

"His eyes are closed now, child."

"Lucy, he was a good father."

"Yes, he was."

"He was always threatening to birch me. And you know what? He never even had a birch rod. He never hit any of us."

"He loved you, child."

"How can I live without him? I don't want to live without him. The way I feel, I want to die too."

"Nobody dies from grief."

"But I want to."

"Lucy ain't gonna let you."

"Where's my mama?"

"She be upstairs with Mrs. Moore. She be all broken up. She gonna be no use to you today. You gotta depend on Lucy."

"You'll stay with me? You won't leave?"

"Yes, I'll stay."

"My father made you free, Lucy. You can go if you want."

"None of us be free, child. When you white folk gonna learn that? We all be tied to sumpthin'."

"I've been mean to you. John Reid scolded me because I was mean to you. So why should you stay?"

"'Cause I wants to."

"Lucy, do you think I'll ever see John again. Or Daniel? Or David?"

"Don't you be thinkin' that way, now. Don't you let your mind turn against you like that. Sure, you will."

"Lucy, Mr. Moore is asking the Hessians if we can bury my father in St. Michael's churchyard. I wonder if they'll move the artillery when we bury him."

# CHAPTER
## 26

We buried my father on Monday, the twenty-third. The ground gave up a coldness that made the air feel like the grave. The guns had been removed from the churchyard, and the detachment of Hessians that stood nearby behaved with utmost respect. I stood very close to Mama. She had spent the last few days in her room, cared for by Lucy and Mrs. Moore. I don't think she knew what was going on. She seemed dim-witted now. She barely ate and her eyes did not look at you, they looked beyond. She seemed almost bewitched.

At the burial she showed no feelings, not even when Betsy Moore hugged her, crying. She seemed not to recognize anyone or even pay mind to the fact that she was in a churchyard. But it was just as well, for when the doors of the church opened, I could see the Hessians' horses stabled inside.

I felt almost relieved that Father was dead and could not see that.

Back at our house the few neighbors we had left had assembled and brought hot soup and cornmeal pudding and cured meats and pies. I sat quietly and ate while people came up to me and said good things about my father and called me a poor child.

"It has a thin coat of ice on it already," Mrs. Potts was saying to Mr. Moore. "It looks as if the Lord is with the British. If the river freezes, they'll be able to walk across it and take Philadelphia."

I hated Mrs. Potts at that moment more than I'd ever hated anyone. As soon as I could, I cornered Mr. Moore.

"Mr. Moore, do you think the Lord is with the British?"

"The day is not over yet, Jemima. I'd wait a while before venturing to say what side the Lord is on. There is a swift current beneath that river. It will stay alive and moving and strong under the coat of ice."

"So will I, Mr. Moore."

He smiled at me. "I would speak with thee, Jemima. We have offered to take thy mother until she comes out of her bereavement. Would thee think of coming home with us?"

"No, sir. I wasn't thinking on it. I'll stay here with Lucy."

"But a young girl and a servant alone in a town occupied by Hessians—"

"We'll be all right, Mr. Moore. The Hessians wouldn't dare bother us. Killing my father was bad enough. You told me yourself how upset Rall was over it."

"We don't know yet that it was these Hessians who killed him, child. Control the hate in thy heart until thee is sure."

"I'm sure. And I hate them for it. I don't care if it's sinful to hate. And I'm staying. If you take Mother, that will give Lucy and me more time to care for the house and the shop."

"The shop!" He was dumbfounded. "Certainly thee can't be thinking of running the shop! I could not, with the affection I have for thy parents, allow—"

"Oh, Mr. Moore, please! It meant so much to my father.

And it would make me feel so much better! It would be like . . . keeping a part of Father alive!"

He was shaking his head. "Two women alone, child."

"The shop is our livelihood, Mr. Moore. Would you have me give it up? And if we leave, the shop will be ransacked again! And the house! I'd die if that happened. You wouldn't want me to die, would you?"

It turned out he didn't want me to die. He summoned Lucy into Father's study, though, and satisfied himself that she was not only devoted but quick-witted and sensible before he would give permission.

"Jemima, thy father often told me that thee was the most difficult one to reason with," he said. "I'll check on thee whenever I can."

Lucy and I were sitting before the fire in the parlor that night when there was a knock on the door. Lucy put a finger to her lips. We waited, but the knocking became a pounding. It kept on until Lucy got up and opened the door.

There were five Hessians—three hulking men dressed in the red and white of the Von Lossberg Regiment and two women who wore coarse clothing.

"You cannot come into this house. We have had a death here." Lucy stood her ground, speaking in perfect English. But they pushed past her and came into the parlor, warming themselves before the fire.

Again Lucy demanded they leave, but they ignored her. I looked over at the fireplace where Father's musket would be, but it had been lost that night when he went out on his mission.

"Leave this house!" I said firmly. "We have friends and they'll be here to check on us."

They only laughed at me. One of the women came toward

me, muttering in a pacifying tone. Then, reaching out, she touched the gold and ivory locket I wore pinned to the front of my short gown. She said something I did not understand. Was she directing me to take it off? I shook my head no. Then she yanked hard and pulled it off, ripping the material of my short gown with it.

I screamed. "Give me that! It's mine!" She slapped me on the face, hard. I reeled and caught myself, and in an instant Lucy was between us, holding onto me.

"How dare you come into this house and behave in such a manner? This is our *home!* Have you no respect?"

The Hessian captain stepped forward and rebuked the woman sharply. She moved back, cringing under his harsh words.

"I want my locket. Give it back to me."

She held it against her bosom. The captain spoke sharply again, and like a child she yielded the locket to me. The captain bowed, speaking in halting English to Lucy. He explained that they had been sent to secure quarters for a British officer and our house was suitable, since it was so nice and large. And he had his orders. The British officer would take possession in a day or so. In the meantime, if we stayed confined to our chambers, no harm would come to us.

The captain himself saw us upstairs. He bowed, assuring us that we had no worries. If we would bolt our door from the inside, we would sleep safely through the night.

Inside my room, I started to cry. "What will we do, Lucy?"

She quieted me, bathing my face and making me undress before I got into bed. Then she lay down next to me and held me, for I was trembling.

"But Lucy, what will we do?"

"We stay together," she said, "and we say our prayers."

I marveled at Lucy's courage. The next morning when we went downstairs, I screamed when I saw Hessian women cutting up dead chickens on Mama's good cherry dining room table. But Lucy just pulled me along to the kitchen. There she directed the Hessians to leave, saying it was her kitchen and that she would make the breakfast. They obeyed.

She set a mug of hot coffee and corn bread down before me. "We don't bother them, no matter what they be doin'. No matter what they take. You hear? Don't be afraid. It be only a house, only furniture, only *things!*"

"I'm not afraid, Lucy."

"Yes, you are. It don't matter bein' afraid. It matters *showin'* them. They won't hurt us."

"How do you know?"

"I knows. Because if they try, I'll kill them."

That day and night the Hessians stayed in our house, and Lucy became my whole sanity and hope. She became my family. It still hurt, though, when the Hessian women went through Mama's linen press and took out her finely woven things, and when they confiscated some of Father's clothes from the bedroom.

When their men came back that night they gathered downstairs, eating and drinking my father's best rum, singing their songs, laughing and banging things around.

Upstairs in our chamber we listened. "They be drunk," Lucy said.

It got cold. We had no more wood for the fire and we'd had no supper. We wrapped ourselves in quilts and listened to the commotion. Laughter resounded through the house. Once or twice something smashed. It sounded as if my mother's whole sideboard crashed to the floor in the dining room.

"Maybe I sneak down and git some food," Lucy said.

"No, Lucy. We do have something." I jumped up and went to my wooden chest, where I'd kept the supply of pemmican Canoe had given me. And so we ate pemmican that night.

At about ten o'clock, there was a knock on the front door. We heard a sharp, clear voice with a British accent, then silence. It got quiet after that, with only the occasional sounds of low conversation.

There were murmurs, exclamations from the Hessians, and then it seemed like an argument between the British and the Hessians. The door banged and we heard the Hessians out in the street. I ran to the window and saw them bundled up, walking away.

"They're leaving, Lucy!" I was jubilant.

"The British," she said, "they come."

I didn't know whether to rejoice or be more worried.

"They be civilized, at least," Lucy said.

"I've heard stories that they're not so civilized sometimes, Lucy."

"We see in the morning. In the morning I be up early. We see about the British."

# CHAPTER
## 27

He was so young. He was as young as Daniel, surely. In the bright sunlight he stood in the middle of our parlor, and the red of his coat sent a shock through me.

The British were in our house.

He was pacing restlessly. He wore snow-white breeches, and his black boots covered his knees in front. His spurs were silver and flashed in the sun, as did the silver fringe on the blue velvet epaulets on his shoulders. His crimson sash was silk, I was sure of it, and his sword had an elaborate silver hilt.

But it was his helmet that frightened me the most. It was made of black leather with red horsehair streaming out from a silver comb on top. On the front plate was the letter *C* and underneath it was written "The Queen's."

He bowed when he saw us and took his helmet off in one sweeping gesture. He was very blond. But before he got a chance to talk, Lucy ran and knelt at his feet.

"Sir, we are two women alone. The Hessians have terrorized us and frightened this poor child, who so recently lost her father. I ask you, sir, I beg you, if you consider yourself civilized, to have mercy on two women whose men have been taken by the war. Restore civility to this Christian home. Allow us to conduct ourselves in a dignified manner and proceed unharmed, and your stay will be most comfortable."

I couldn't believe those words were coming out of Lucy! The sun streamed in on the fair hair of the handsome young British officer as he looked down on her. He reached out and touched her shoulder. "Where is your mistress?"

"She is with friends, sir. She is bereaved and in shock after the death of her husband. But I am a free woman."

"Get on your feet. I want no woman kneeling before me, free or otherwise."

Lucy stood.

"Who, then, is the mistress of this house?"

"Jemima Emerson." Lucy turned toward me. "I am in her employ."

He drew himself to attention, with his strange black helmet tucked under one arm. "Miss, may I present myself. I am Captain Andrew Bygrave of the Sixteenth Light Dragoons. I apologize for the intrusion and offer condolences for the death of your father and for the wanton destruction of your house. I shall have the Hessians come back to restore it to its former condition. We are stationed at the Friends Meeting House, but my commanding officer, Lieutenant Colonel William Harcourt, requests the use of your home for a day and a night. He needs a warm fire, some decent food, and a place of quietude to confer with his officers. In return, on my word as an officer in His Majesty's army, I promise you the right to move about freely. You and your maidservant shall be accorded the utmost respect and protection."

He finished his speech and waited. I studied the handsome face, but his feelings were well concealed.

"You can't be more than twenty," I said.

"I was at Brooklyn Heights and White Plains, miss. I've seen my share of fighting."

"I have a brother your age. He's away fighting. But the last I saw him, he looked very ragged. You have fine clothes and boots. I have a dear friend who is close to death in north Jersey, who was on the retreat with Washington."

"I'm deeply sorry for that, miss."

"How can you be? How can you know how it feels to have someone you have cared about and grown up with, dying?"

"I believe I do somewhat, miss. I lost my brother at Breed's Hill."

I didn't know what to say then. And for the first time I saw a flicker of emotion in his face.

"You may stay," I said. "You're probably better than the Hessians. Although that remains to be seen."

He bowed again and relaxed. "Do you have any food, miss? Could your maidservant fetch me a bit of breakfast? And perhaps, later, some supper for my commanding officer? We're a long way from home, and it is Christmas Day."

I had forgotten that it was Christmas Day! Had my family been home we would have gone to church and had a fine feast afterward. I couldn't help remembering last Christmas when Mama and Lucy had prepared food for days and Raymond Moore had asked me to write to him and John Reid had toasted me. How long ago it seemed!

At ten that morning, after he had breakfasted, our young captain was about to leave for parade-and-inspection when there was a knock on the door. He answered it. I heard him talking for a moment; then he came to the kitchen, where

I was helping Lucy with the cooking.

"A note for you, miss. Delivered by Mr. Potts's servant."

I stared at it, shaking. From John? Impossible! Who, then? I accepted the note, and he stood and waited while I read it.

It was from the Moores. They had received word that Raymond had died. Mr. Moore was on his way north to bring home the body. My mother was doing fine, they wrote, and soon I would be able to come and see her. Ruth and Betsy would care for the place until Mr. Moore returned.

I crumpled it up, the tears coming down my face. The young captain stepped forward. "May I be of help?"

"What is it, child?" Lucy asked. I gave the note to her.

"I'm all right," I told Captain Bygrave. "My friend, the one I told you about, has died."

"I'm so very sorry. If there is anything I can do..."

"Do?" I stared at him. "You've done it all! You have done all you can do. To all of us!"

He stepped back, white-faced, as if I had struck him. He turned on his heel and walked out.

True to his word, the Hessians returned and straightened the house while he was gone. When he came back at two with his commanding officer and two brother officers, the house was in order and the Hessians were gone. The officers went straight to the parlor, where Lucy had a fire laid. When she went in to bring brandy and a light repast, I followed and got a glimpse of them lounging on our chairs, their fine red coats open in front.

"God, this is a finely appointed house," I heard one of them say. "Makes one feel almost civilized again."

I ran back to the kitchen and kneaded my dough. Tears

were falling from my face a few moments later when the captain appeared.

"I wish to speak to Miss Emerson."

Lucy nodded, and he came to the table. "You're crying. I'll leave if my presence so distresses you."

"It isn't you. I mean, not you yourself. It's just..."

"I understand. I came to ask if you would sup with us this evening. My commanding officer wishes me to ask."

"I think not."

"It is Christmas Day. You would honor us."

"I don't wish to honor you, sir."

I saw him quickly conceal the disappointment in his face. He bowed slightly. "If there is anything I can do for you, please let me know." He started to walk away.

"Captain."

"Yes?"

"You could. A little matter. But it would mean much to me."

"Well?"

"You have a horse in our barn."

"We took the freedom of stabling our horses in your barn, yes."

"If I could pay him a visit."

He frowned.

"I had a horse and we had to send him away. I miss him dearly. We have our carriage horses but they aren't the same. I could bring yours some dried apple."

I saw the hint of a smile in his face. "My horse is in the last stall," he said. Then he turned and left.

His horse was black, and I was surprised to see that it was fully harnessed. It whinnied and nuzzled me as I approached, grateful for companionship. I gave it dried apple and patted its silken head.

"Where did you come from?" I murmured. The closeness of it, its sounds and smells, all reminded me of Bleu. I stood patting it, letting the hot tears come down my face. From where I stood, I could see the officers having their after-supper coffee in the light of the oil lamps in our parlor.

I wanted my father to be in the parlor. I wanted to go in and find him there with my mother and John Reid.

"Did you come all the way across the sea to visit me?" Talking to the horse eased my misery.

"He came on a horse boat. The trip took four months. And the rotting transport I came over on was not much better."

The young British officer was standing, hatless, his coat open, a glass of wine in his hand, watching me rather unsteadily. I felt a shiver of fear. He was not yet drunk but had a pleasant sort of haziness about him. He moved closer.

"We're both here only since July, in case you were wondering."

"I wasn't."

"I've been drinking, yes. It eases my misery, but you needn't be afraid. I've no intention of harming you."

"I wasn't afraid."

"Yes, you were. I saw it in your eyes a moment ago. You're heard stories about us ravishing women. Don't you think, if I were going to ravish you, I would have tried it already?"

I said nothing.

"I'm not the kind who ravishes women. Anyway, I've a sister your age. She's a dear child, and I hadn't realized how much I missed her until I met you."

"I have two brothers. And I miss them every day."

We fell silent.

"What's your horse's name?" I asked.

"Cicero."

"Why do you keep him fully harnessed?"

"Orders. We must be in readiness at all times. Colonel Rall has been advised that the Americans might attack, but he considers it old women's talk. Still, we must be in readiness."

The Americans attack! I felt a thrill, but I kept my voice normal. "His blanket is very handsome."

"Did you ride your horse much when you had him?"

"Every day. My grandfather gave him to me. He's away now, helping to put down an Indian uprising."

"This is a strange and wild country. Sometimes I wonder what in God's name I'm doing here, thousands of miles from home."

"It's a fine country. It's ours and we . . . we mean to keep it," I told him firmly. "You'll find that out."

"My, you're a dyed-in-the-wool Rebel, aren't you?"

"I just wanted to tell you what to expect."

"I know what to expect. The Americans can fight. They've simply had a streak of bad luck. I heard what they did at Breed's Hill. Anyone who underestimates them is a fool."

"Have your superiors underestimated them?"

He drained his glass of wine. "General Howe was advised at Long Island that Washington was retreating, and he took his sweet time before giving orders to advance. And Cornwallis had orders from Howe not to advance beyond New Brunswick. Howe was content to keep East Jersey. Then Cornwallis delayed seventeen hours at Princeton when he should have been pursuing Washington. He took a whole day to march twelve hours to Trenton. Had he not delayed, we would have had the Americans before they crossed the river."

He looked at me darkly, "Your precious army is safe across

the river, either because Howe is a fool or he takes special delight in allowing Washington to elude him. And Rall is an ass. Early this week he was told about the movements of the American army. He said, 'Let them come.'"

I could scarcely breathe lest it break the spell. He was leaning against the stall, quite miserable.

"I don't mind being here in a strange land. Even though I know I'll probably die here as my brother did. I don't mind that it's an unpopular war at home, that you Americans have many sympathizers in Parliament. What I mind is fighting under commanders whose pride comes first, over common sense."

He stood straight and looked at me. "I could be court-martialed for what I just said to you."

"You could only be court-martialed if it's repeated."

"I'm loyal to my King." There were tears in his eyes.

"I'm sure you are."

He smiled at me and I smiled back. "I'm sorry for what I said about this being a strange and wild country."

"And I'm sorry for how I offended you this morning when you offered me your sympathy."

"We're even, then."

"It is a strange and wild country. But we are very civilized. You should meet my sister. She's most proper. You'd like her."

"I like you." He said it so low that I could barely hear it. I was numb with shock. John Reid had known me over two years before he'd uttered those words.

"I've offended you."

"You must understand. I have brothers and someone I care for, off fighting. My father was killed by the Hessians. I shouldn't even be here talking to you."

"But you are."

Yes, I was. I thought of John and what he would say, how he would scold me for getting into something again. The thought of him made my head clear. The young captain had been kind. I didn't hate him as I supposed I should. There was no sense in lying to myself. There for a moment I'd been drawn to him. How *could* I? How could I be so despicable? It made no sense.

But how could he be the enemy and be kind? That made less sense than anything. "I must go in," I said.

"I've made you uncomfortable. But I wanted you to know that our being on opposite sides doesn't preclude my having . . . feelings for you. I find American girls have a spirit and honesty about them that is most refreshing."

"Then let me be honest, sir, and say that I appreciate your kindness and your decency and shall remember you always for it. But now I must go in."

He bowed, took my arm, and walked me to the house.

# CHAPTER
## 28

I had just gone to my chamber at eight o'clock when there was a great commotion in the street, with men shouting and running. Someone pounded on our door. I ran into the hall to hear Lieutenant Colonel Harcourt and the British captain discussing it.

". . . a raid at the picket post on Penny Town Road. Four wounded," I heard Harcourt say.

Lucy came upstairs, shushing me and pushing me back into my chamber. "Could be an attack. Leastways that's what they is sayin'. We stay in here."

I looked out my window to see the British dragoons mounted on their horses. They conferred for a moment and rode off. The young captain rode his horse very well.

The street outside settled under the silence of thick, falling snow. I woke in a few hours to hear the British come back in with a clamor. One of them cursed. Another yelled. "By God, it's still Christmas! Let's have a toast!"

I lay in bed listening to them toast King George the

Third. Next they toasted the British Parliament. Then they toasted General Howe.

The attack must have been a false alarm, Lucy said. I could barely contain my disappointment. But I slept again. And this time I didn't wake until an hour after dawn, when the real attack began.

I was awakened by the clock in the hall chiming and a cannon going off in the muffled distance. The clock stopped, but the cannon didn't.

I jumped out of bed, half dazed. The cannon went off again, closer. I felt it sound in my bones.

Where was Lucy? The next thing I knew she was gliding toward me in the half light. "Get dressed."

"Lucy, what is it?"

"The Americans. They be attackin'."

Then there came a pounding on our front door. Downstairs the British were scurrying about, cursing loudly, "By God," an English voice boomed. "I knew it!"

I dressed. Doors slammed downstairs, and in a few minutes horses' hooves galloped around our house and into the street. The snow was mixed with sleet out on Queen Street. The British dragoons galloped toward the Assunpink Creek south of town. A group of Hessians came out of a house across the street, half dressed, hailing them down. They did not stop. They almost ran the Hessians over.

Lucy wanted to go into the cellar, but I refused. "This is my house, Lucy. I won't hide in the cellar like a rat. I want to know what's going on around me."

She gave me no argument, perhaps because she wanted to see what was going on too. "You jes' stay away from those windows," she directed. "I be goin' down to make some breakfast. We might as well git some vittles in us. The Good Lord knows when we be eatin' again."

But I ran from window to window to find out what was happening. All I could see was smoke over on King Street and swirling snow. I could hear shouting in the distance, the breaking of glass, the whinnying of horses, the musket and cannon fire. And it was coming closer.

There was the awful sound of the beating-to-arms, the drumming that called the men to order, which anyone would recognize if they had a soul, no matter what side they were on. The battle seemed to be raging all around us. Hessians were still pouring out of houses on Queen Street, waving their arms and going back inside again.

Down the street came more British dragoons. They raced toward the bridge at the end of town. I knelt on the window seat trying to see up Front Street. I counted eight cannon being dragged by Americans. My heart nearly burst inside, watching them. Then I felt someone put a blanket around my shoulders.

"Come 'n' eat."

"Lucy, I want to find Daniel. He must be with them." And John, I thought, but I couldn't tell her that. She still thought he was a Tory.

"Daniel's a big boy. He be findin' his way home."

"But we just can't sit here!"

"You'll get kilt out there, and Lucy ain't gonna allow it."

The Hessians were pouring down our street, trying to form some kind of order. No, they were trying to get out of town. They were running wildly up Queen, then coming back again. The Americans must have the cannon on the bridge over the Assunpink, I decided. They must be blocking the way out of town.

The cannon boomed, the drums beat, and it was all muffled by falling snow. From Daniel's room in back of the house I saw Hessians forming on King Street with their artillery. In the next moment I heard a roar that seemed to shatter my bones. Then horses screamed and I saw men go down. But because of the snow, it all had a far-off quality. Sometimes I could not even make out the color of the uniforms or see who was falling down.

Only three quarters of an hour had gone by since the battle started. About a block up on Queen Street I saw half a dozen Hessians on horseback followed by several hundred men. The one leading must be Colonel Rall, I decided. I watched them turn up Quaker Lane and take Fourth Street to march out of town.

I heard another roar, but it was not cannon. It was the unmistakable roar of human voices, as if thousands of maddened souls had been let loose. American soldiers were darting in between houses in ones and twos, skeletonlike, coming out of the snow. They looked crazed, with their clothes in tatters and their faces covered with mud. I could follow them by the puffs of smoke from the firing of their muskets.

The snow blew across my line of vision and blocked everything out like a curtain. Then it cleared again. In the distance I saw a figure on a dark horse wearing deep blue. It stood out from the others. Mounted officers followed it and then the long, tattered line of men.

Washington!

I could barely breathe. The snow swirled again, closing around the Americans. I wanted to cry. The Hessians were in the distance in a meadow off Fourth Street. In the next few minutes everything got confused, and they all looked like little miniatures moving on the white stage before my eyes.

I saw the man in the dark blue go down and his horse

roll to the ground. Then, amid the distant sounds of battle, men were running and falling while cannon fired. This continued for five more minutes, and then everything stopped.

It got quiet. All I could hear was the sound of the snow as it piled up on my window.

I went downstairs. Lucy was cooking. The smell of fresh-baked bread was in the kitchen, and I realized I was hungry. "Sit down 'n' eat," she directed.

I sat and drank some coffee and ate bread and honey. There was a knock on the front door. We looked at each other. She waved me to silence and went to answer it. I ventured into the hall, listening.

It was the servant girl from Stacy Potts's house. The battle was over, the girl said. The Americans had taken Trenton. They had lost no one. Colonel Rall, the Hessian commander, had been shot.

Still, Lucy would not let me go out.

"I want to find my brothers. Lucy, I'll die if they're in town and I don't see them!"

"Supposin' I lets you go out in them streets and they come here? Cap'n Dan would kill me iff'n I lets you roam them streets with them men out there. Now go git me some eggs from the buttery."

She kept me in the house. All up and down Queen Street I could hear the voices and sounds of men and horses. I peeked out the front windows, wondering if any soldiers would come to our door. But they were busy stacking captured goods, blankets, muskets, coats, and barrels of dry stuffs. Some men just sank wearily down on the wooden walks, unable to move farther.

They herded the Hessians into groups. Hatless and un-armed, they did not look like the fierce soldiers Rall had paraded through our streets. They looked uncertain, like the rest of us, as if some seam had unraveled and come undone inside them.

There was a knock on our door about half an hour later, and I went to open it. A soldier stood there with long wet hair that had come undone from his queue and half covered his face, which was blackened from gunpowder. He was covered with mud, yet not so much that I couldn't make out that the coat had once been red and blue.

"Will you come in?" I started to say, "We have food. And there's coffee. Do you have anyone with you?"

Then I saw his sword and noticed there was something familiar about his shoulders as he leaned against the door, looking as if he would fall over in a dead faint.

"I'm Daniel, Jem," he said.

# CHAPTER
## 29

"How are you, Jem?"

He was as confident and commanding a presence as ever, despite his bedraggled appearance. I reached out to him. "No, no, Jem, I'm filthy. Wait until I clean up a bit. Are you all right? Is everyone all right?"

But I couldn't answer. I stood there staring at him as if I were suddenly dim-witted.

"In heaven's name, Jem, has the war made you daft? Come along then."

I followed him through the hall. Lucy stood in the door of the kitchen. "Welcome home, Cap'n Daniel."

"Hello, Lucy." In the kitchen he removed his sword and pistols, his hat and coat. He took the piece of flannel she offered him and washed his hands and face and tied his hair back. Then he opened his arms to me.

His embrace was fierce. "Jem, why are you crying?" He drew back, looked around the empty kitchen and saw the stricken look on Lucy's face.

"Where are Mother and Father?" he said.

He sat next to the kitchen fire and sipped his mug of

coffee while we told him all that had happened. His face went very white, and he listened without saying a word. I saw tears come to his eyes, but he held them in check. And then I saw his jaw set forever in the ways of a man.

"So, the Hessians were here. And the British. And they did you no harm?"

"No, sir," Lucy said.

"Jem?" He looked at me.

"They did me no harm, Dan."

"Where..." He cleared his throat. "Where is Father buried?"

"In St. Michael's churchyard," I said.

"And Mama is with the Moores, you say."

"Yes. She hasn't been right since it happened. The Moores want to keep her and nurse her. I wanted to go there, but I didn't have the chance. Perhaps I will now."

He heard the tremor in my voice, saw my pain, and saw through it to something else. "My poor Jem. Lucy, would you see if you could get my coat a little clean, please? I have a meeting in an hour." He picked up his sword and pistols. "Come along, Jem, we can talk in the parlor."

He closed the door behind us, set down the sword and pistols, and put his mug on the mantel. He seemed so much taller. His face had a day's worth of beard and he looked tired, but the aura of authority about him was unmistakable. "Good Lord, Jem, I'm twenty-one and I'm the head of a family. Well, it can't be any worse than leading a rag-tailed regiment in a retreat across the Jerseys. How is Betsy?"

"The Moores wrote that they were well. They've lost Raymond and Mr. Moore has gone to...fetch him home."

A shadow crossed his face. "I expected it. I blame myself. If I hadn't asked to have him with me when I came south..."

"It isn't your fault."

"You were writing to him. Were you two—"

"No, Dan. I was fond of Raymond, but we ended up just being friends."

"Then who is it? Come, now, don't pretend innocence. I haven't time for games. I don't even have time to see Mother. I have an idea we'll be crossing back into Pennsylvania before this day is up, and I must be off soon."

"It's John Reid, Dan. But how did you know?"

He showed no surprise. "I should hope I've had enough experience with my men to know when someone is aching to ask me something. John, is it?" He smiled. "I must say I'm glad of it. So you two managed to stop fighting long enough to realize you loved each other. When did you last hear from him?"

"He was here on the thirteenth, on a mission."

He nodded. "That would be right. He also could have been one of the volunteers in farmer's clothing who preceded our march this morning. They were to reconnoiter Hessian outposts and prevent Tories from carrying warnings."

"You mean he might be here today?"

"No, Jem. If he was one of them he wouldn't show his face in town until it's safe for a Tory. He took enough of a chance being recognized this morning. My guess is he'll want to keep his Tory identity and you'll be hearing from him when you least expect it." He smiled. "Or I will, most likely, when he discovers I'm the one he has to ask for your hand."

"And what will you say?"

"I'll tell him I'll give you a substantial dowry and wish him well. With you, Jem, he'll need all my best wishes. Come along, you can walk through town with me before my meeting." He put on his pistols and we went to the kitchen, where Lucy had his coat brushed and dried.

"Beautiful, Lucy." He put on the coat and the sword. "I know you're dying to know about Cornelius. I haven't seen him. Or David." He turned to me. "The last I knew they were supposed to cross nine miles below town with General Cadwalader. As far as I know they haven't shown. But I'm sure they're all right."

"Dan, Lucy is free now. Father freed her and Cornelius before . . . the British and Hessians came to town."

"Wonderful, Lucy. I'm so glad." He reached out and took her hand. "You'll stay on, I hope. I'll pay you whatever you ask to stay and look out for Jem in my absence."

Soldiers saluted Dan as we walked through town. Once or twice he stopped to nudge some poor weary soldier who was drunk from confiscated rum. He'd scold him, bawl him out, and send him on his way, but gently. "They can't be faulted," he said. "They've won their first battle in months—and against the most powerful army in the world. Do you know what it means, Jem? We were retreating for months. We were beaten. It was all lost and so hopeless, and then Washington decided to take this chance."

He told me about the crossing in the sleet and dark, with the ice floes on the river hitting the boats, about the endless march, of having to keep his men's spirits up. "Washington was everywhere, it seemed, encouraging us."

There was a crowd in front of Stacy Potts's house. Dan took my arm. "There, Jem, now you can see him. It's Washington."

I scarcely saw the two men with him. My eyes were drawn to the man in the dark blue cloak as if I were bewitched. I saw the way he strode through the lines of Pennsylvania Riflemen, who parted ranks, the way his cloak swung open to reveal his buff breeches and sword, his stature, the breadth of his shoulders, the way he turned before going into the Potts's house, his eyes briefly surveying the crowd.

A silence fell over everyone. For a moment he seemed to look right in my direction. I felt a sort of calm come over me as I saw the look on his face. For there was a sternness, a forbidding manner that made one cringe and remember all one's sins. And then, just as one was about to despair, there was a kindness in his eyes, lighting the way for a steady, strong compassion that came from within that I would remember for the rest of my days.

Colonel Rall died that day in Stacy Potts's house. Our army left town late that afternoon, with over a thousand Hessian prisoners. Dan had given me permission to run Father's shop. For the first time that night I felt at peace. John Reid would be coming back soon, I was sure of it.

# CHAPTER
## *30*

Almost two thousand American soldiers were back in Trenton on the last day of the year, concentrated on the banks of the Assunpink Creek.

Lucy and I had no idea what was going on. There was all sorts of activity outside, and someone told us that General Washington had taken up headquarters in the home of Major Barnes, which was right up the street from us.

At nine there was a knock on our door. It was Daniel. He stepped in out of the cold with another officer. "This is Lieutenant Edward Rawlings, a friend of mine. My sister, lieutenant."

The lieutenant was tall and rangy, and he bowed. I remembered to curtsy. "Have you any hot coffee?" Dan asked. "We've just traveled that nine miles for the third time in a week."

In the kitchen Dan told us that Washington was reestablishing himself in New Jersey and that the British were marshaling forces in Princeton. "I've only an hour before I must get back. I've come to tell you to pack up and take the wagon to the Moores'. Plan to stay for a day or so. It looks like another battle is shaping up."

"Oh, Dan, we were all right in the last one. I don't want to leave!"

He turned, mug in hand. "Do you hear that, lieutenant? Didn't I tell you? Jemima Emerson, you have exactly half an hour to pack your things. Lucy will help you. The lieutenant and I will shut up the house and hitch up the team. If you think I'm going to be out there worrying about this house getting hit by cannon fire with you two in it . . . or what will happen if we don't win this battle . . ." He paused. "I warn you, miss, I'm not accustomed to having my orders disobeyed."

The lieutenant stood up. "I'd do as he says, miss. He gets powerful mad when you give him an argument."

But he's only my brother, I wanted to say. Then I saw the look on Dan's face and I didn't say it. Lucy and I went to pack.

Dan and the lieutenant accompanied us on horseback to the banks of the Assunpink, where the army was standing in formation. David and Cornelius were somewhere in its midst, but it was impossible to spot them. We stopped. Dan dismounted and helped me down. We walked a bit away from the wagon. "Here are two notes. One for Betsy. And one for you from John."

I gave a small cry. He hushed me. "He slipped into our camp across the river last night in the disguise of a farmer selling tobacco. I told him about Father's death. He was devastated. He thought much of Father. And there in the dark, while he sold me tobacco, he asked for your hand."

He smiled. "He said he had intended to wait, but Father's

death changed things and he didn't know when we'd meet again. I said yes. So you're betrothed. He said he wouldn't marry yet, not until he's finished with certain work. I'm sure you'll hear from him soon. He's very busy. Go along now and give my love to Mother."

I looked up at him. How well he'd taken Father's place in the last few days! "Thank you, Dan. Do take care."

"I'll be fine. I'll write." He kissed me, mounted Gulliver, and rode off to join the troops.

We sat watching. A very heavy young officer on a noble-looking horse was addressing the troops. From Dan's description, he would be Henry Knox, who had once been a bookseller and who had brought the cannon down from Fort Ticonderoga. His words rang out in the cold air. He was urging the men to stay on a few days longer since enlistments were up this last day of 1776.

When he finished, Washington spoke. He told them they had served with great fidelity and that they had a right to be discharged. And then he begged them to stay. He promised them a bounty of ten dollars each from his own private fortune for another six weeks of service. He begged them to look at the position in which they would place the cause of liberty if they left now. All would be for naught, he said, if they did not attempt to check the advance of the foe. He stopped speaking. The silence that followed was terrifying. Somebody coughed. General Washington's horse moved its head restlessly.

Then one or two of the soldiers, like ragged scarecrows, poised their firelocks to signify their willingness to stay. One after another, the others followed. And if there were tears on General Washington's face, I could not see for the tears on my own.

"Come on, Lucy, let's go," I said.

My dearest:

Please don't worry about me. I am doing what
I want to do and have thus far been successful. I
have seen your brother and scribble this note by
firelight to tell you he has given permission for
our betrothal. He has been more than generous in
giving you a dowry, and says he will write the
necessary letters for its arrangement to your
grandfather Henshaw in Philadelphia as soon as
he can. I have been offered a commission in the
American army and, at Dan's urging, have decided
to take it. It will be a help in my work if for no
other reason than I'll have decent clothes to wear.
What could be warmer this winter than the uniform of an American officer? I rejoice in the victory at Trenton. There will be others. I have had
to say goodbye to my friend, Charles Apgar, in
Philadelphia since I shan't need to see him once I
accept my commission. I shall write to you. My
deepest regrets about your father. I know how he
loved you. Remember all I have taught you.

Your obedient servant and loving intended.

John

I could barely see the road ahead for my tears. As usual,
I had to decipher much of his meaning, but this wasn't
difficult. He was joining the American army to have the
protection of a uniform in case he was picked up on any
future missions. That way he would only be taken prisoner
and not hung as a spy. He would not be placing ads in the
Philadelphia newspaper anymore. He would write directly
to me as would any officer in the American army. My heart
was so full as Lucy drove the wagon to the Moores'. A

commission in the American army! Now, wasn't that fine!
And then there was Daniel, arranging for my dowry before
he went off to the next battle. A girl never had a more
bittersweet bethrothal, I was sure of it.

"Mama?"

She was sitting in the Moores' parlor, hemming an apron
and humming a little song to herself. Hesitantly, I walked
in. The sun splashed in the window onto her lap as her
slender hands worked the stitches.

"Hello, Mama, how are you?"

She looked up at me and smiled. But in the blue eyes
there was no recognition. There was peace and content-
ment, such as I had not seen in those eyes for months. But
she did not know me.

"Do you like it?" She was embroidering the letter *E* on
the corner of the apron. And I remembered how, in the
past few months, she and her Society ladies had made coats
for the army and stitched the name of the lady who had
sewed the coat, and the town, inside.

"It's beautiful," I said.

"Dear, you look as if you could use a new apron. The
one you have on is rather worn. Doesn't your mama mind
when you go out like that?"

I thought my heart would burst inside me. I looked down
at my apron, which I had forgotten to take off when leaving.
I felt my head spin and thought I would faint. Dear God,
I said to myself, David is somewhere with that army out
there. And Daniel is there, preparing for battle. Father is
dead, I don't know when I'll see John again, and my own
mother doesn't know me.

"My mama doesn't know I'm out looking like this," I

said, "and I'd love to have a new apron. Would you make me one?"

At five in the afternoon we heard the cannon fire from the Moore house. It continued through dusk but shortly after dark it stopped.

Betsy and I watched from her chamber upstairs. When it got quiet, I looked at her.

"What do you think has happened, Betsy?"

"I don't know. Didn't thee say our army was on the high ground?"

"Yes."

"Well, look, the fires still burn there."

She was right. She went down to help her mother feed the livestock, for her father hadn't returned yet. Only then did I realize that she had referred to the Americans as "our army." I went to sleep that night comforted by the sight of those fires.

In the morning, after breakfast, I convinced Lucy to take me home. When we got back we were told that during the night our army had slipped out of town. The campfires had been decoys to fool the British! Rumors flew around town. Some said the Americans had wrapped rags around their wagon wheels so the British wouldn't hear them leave during the night. But no one knew where they went, not even the surgeons working for Washington who came to tend the wounded.

# CHAPTER
## *31*

The war left us, finally. I speak of the one with the guns and the shooting, for I discovered that there was terror in our lives that could be equal to war. After the war went, my fears did not leave me.

I had new things to worry about. I wanted to keep the shop open, but I feared I wouldn't be able to get enough supplies. And if I shut it down, it would be like another death in the family.

There was talk that General Howe was going to blockade the whole coast. The southern colonies were still importing powder, arms, clothing, rum, and sugar from Saint Eustatius and Bermuda. There was talk that if Howe succeeded with his blockade, it would break the American rebellion.

I did not know what to think. Men had flocked to the colors after the victories at Trenton and Princeton, but in the spring of 1777 the British still held New York, Perth Amboy, New Brunswick, and Newark. Our army was in Morristown.

I worried about inflation. Last year, according to Father's books, flax was seven pence a pound. Now it was fourteen.

The price of tobacco had risen, and there was no reason to believe it would stop. Planters were talking of thirty shillings per hundredweight.

Molasses was forty-eight dollars a gallon and coffee twelve dollars a pound. The rising price of cotton was exceeded only by that of pepper and rum, all items that I carried when I could get them. And I could not get salt, even with saltworks right in New Jersey at Egg Harbor. The army needed it to cure its meats. I could not keep cotton in the shop. Small supplies came in to Philadelphia from Port-au-Prince, but the shipments were never big enough to satisfy the demand. And the army got first choice of everything.

In February David wrote to me from Morristown saying he had killed two British soldiers at the Battle of Princeton, which they had fought on January 3. "I'll get a few more before I'm finished," he wrote, "to avenge the death of Father."

Then a letter came from Daniel, also at Morristown, saying he was fine but concerned about David's need to kill. Now I had something else to worry me—dear brother David, always so anxious to prove himself a man.

John wrote to me in the beginning of February when he got his commission. He was dispatched on a special mission by the American army. He could not tell me where or when I would hear from him again, but if I did not hear, I was not to despair. If he was caught, he would not be hanged, for he was now in uniform. Since officers were often freed on parole—released from confinement and allowed to move about within limits—I would hear from him if he was captured.

This news didn't make me feel any better, however. I went to see Mama once a week at the Moores', and that only made me feel worse, for she still didn't know me.

I did not hear from John for almost two months, but finally in April a letter came from New York City. He had been picked up by British cavalry in Perth Amboy and sent, as a prisoner of war, to New York. He could move about freely but he had to give his word of honor that he would not try to escape. I should not worry. He was fine.

I had turned seventeen in March, and my father was dead and my family scattered. All I had was Lucy and the shop. And then, in early May, Rebeckah came home with a baby. My fears took a new direction and my worries a new shape.

"Hello, Rebeckah."

She stood in the hall in rustling crimson silk, the sunlight dancing off its silver trim, baggage and baskets surrounding her. I felt shabby and poor in my coarse clothes, with my uncared-for hands. The child in her arms was sleeping.

"How are you, Jem?"

"I'm faring well."

"Well?" She went straight to the parlor and set the child down on the sofa. "How can you be well? You look frightful. Come here and let me look at you."

She studied me closely. "No one who looks as you do can be faring well. Child, you look frazzled."

"I'm not a child anymore, Becky."

She searched my face for evidence that I was being my old saucy self. "No, you aren't, are you? I heard of your betrothal to John Reid. Grandfather Henshaw wrote me from Philadelphia. This happened right after Father's death, I understand. Am I right?"

"And what of it?"

"And Mother gone out of her senses."

I felt the anger rushing through me at her accusations

"Nothing improper has gone on, Becky. Daniel has given his permission. As head of the family, he's very happy about it."

"He would be." She smiled. "Well, you and John Reid. I can't picture it."

"Then don't."

She stiffened. "Where is he?"

"He's in New York, a prisoner of the British. He's an officer in the Continental army."

"John Reid?" She laughed. "John Reid is a Tory."

"He isn't anymore."

"So. He changed his politics for you."

"Not for me, Becky. For himself."

"Oh dear, everything is so different." She looked around the parlor. "Father dead and Mother gone daft from the war. Well, the house still looks decent enough, I will say. But where is the cradle? I wrote and told you to have it ready."

"I received no letter from you, Becky. I didn't know you were coming, or that you had a child."

"Oh, I do have a child. This is Oliver Blakely the Second, who is exactly six weeks old. Last June when General Howe returned to Staten Island I left Philadelphia and met Oliver in New York. He was assigned there."

"He's so tiny."

"Yes, and I am so exhausted. The stage ride was ghastly. My maidservant became ill at Elizabethtown. I was counting on Lucy to be here with open arms. And tea. Where is Lucy?"

"She's in the shop. She works very hard to help me there."

"So you're doing it, aren't you? Daniel wrote Grandfather that he'd given you permission to keep it open. You always did get your own way in this family, Jemima. You're mad, running the shop. You know that, don't you?"

"I haven't had time to consider the question."

"Why are you doing it? There's more than enough money to keep you and Mama comfortable. I know how generous Daniel can be."

"It's more than money. If I can keep the shop open until David gets back, he can take it over. The customers depend on us. And it's part of Father, still living."

"It sounds terribly romantic, but no respectable young woman runs a shop alone. It just isn't proper."

"There's a war on, Becky!"

"Oh, don't remind me. I am sick to the teeth of this endless, dragging, ridiculous war! I was bounced all over the roads in that stage for nearly a week. New York is ghastly. Have you ever tried living in a garrison town? There is nothing to be had to make life decent. Then Oliver suggested I come home after the baby was born. I made the journey as soon as I was up to it. Where *is* Lucy?"

"I'll call her in. She can get the cradle. Do calm down Becky. We don't have tea, but Lucy can fix you coffee."

"Coffee! Oh no, Jemima Emerson, don't you dare tell me you still don't have tea in this house."

"We haven't had it for years, Becky."

"Well, I'm home now, and I will have it. Have Lucy bring some in from the shop."

"We don't stock it in the shop either."

She looked exasperated. "I am here, Jemima Emerson. I am home. I have had enough of this insane war. And I will have my tea. You and Lucy can drink your precious coffee until it comes out of your ears. Life is not bearable without tea. Do you understand?"

"Life has not been bearable for a long time, Becky. Not since Father was killed."

She sighed. "Oh, I still can't believe it! Father dead. Mother out of her senses. And for what? I ask you. All for tea. Do you realize that's what started this whole mess? The stupid tea?"

"It was more than that, Becky."

"More? More?" She looked as if she were going to kill me for a moment, and I became frightened, the way I used to when she'd put the fear of God into me in the old days. But only for a moment.

I drew myself up straight. "We shouldn't discuss politics," I said. "I'll ask Lucy to get the cradle and put up some coffee."

# CHAPTER

## 32

"Mama, Becky has a baby now, an adorable little boy."

I watched her eyes closely, but they were dead. How could that be? How could she not care about her first grandchild?

I had gotten Bleu back from Otter Hall in March and twice a week rode to the Moores' to see my mother. But it pained me every time I went. I couldn't stand seeing her as she was, still under her spell of grief. She had always been busy, attending to seven things at once, running the house, managing everything. I needed her so desperately, and she was not there for me.

What right had she to melt away like a candle in front of my eyes? I was just about an orphan now, with Grandfather Emerson and Daniel away. I was growing, I needed new clothes, it was spring and time for a garden. And all I had was Lucy to help me, and she was so overworked, she never even knew what was going on.

If Becky had gone and seen Mother, that might have helped, but Becky wouldn't go. She was comfortably settled in Mother and Father's room, and she pleaded headaches every time I suggested she pay Mama a visit.

Headaches from what? From afternoons of visiting with her Tory women friends? She'd been having tea in the parlor with two of them when I'd left. Tea! In our house!

The fragrance of it had nearly driven me wild. She drank it in front of me at the table, too. The first time she did it, how my mouth had watered! My very eyes had teared!

All day long I worked in the shop, which accounted for the fact that Becky and I had not yet come to blows. We didn't see each other that much. In the evening she insisted on a formal supper. She had an indentured servant girl now to care for her clothes and the baby. The girl was fourteen and terrified of her.

"Mama, the baby's name is Oliver James."

Still nothing. "Perhaps Becky will let me bring him sometime."

She went on with her stitching. She was making a chemise. I didn't know who it was for, but I sure could have used a new one myself.

"Mama, I'm betrothed to John Reid." I was sure that would elicit a response. She had always loved John so. Hadn't she been the one to always bring up his name to me? I had been too young at the time to realize that both she and Father had wanted John for me long before I wanted him myself.

She held the chemise up for my inspection. "It's beautiful," I said. "Your stitches are so fine."

"You look as if you could use a new one, child. Would you like me to make one for you?"

"Oh, I'd love that." She'd given me the apron she had made. What would I tell people if they asked? My mama made this for me, only she doesn't know she's my mama?

Each time I left the Moores', I felt so confused inside it

took me two days to sort everything out. And then it was time to see Mama again.

I kissed the top of her head. "I have to go, Mama." As always, there were tears in my eyes when I walked out.

In May another letter came from John. He said he was fine and taking full advantage of his parole. I could write to him, provided I remembered everything he had taught me and was especially careful of my penmanship. For he had told the British who opened his mail that his pupil might be writing to him. They very much enjoyed the story of how we were now betrothed, and he did not want them to see a sloppy letter, so I should be careful in my writing.

I knew that he meant that I must not say anything to give him away, for he was still carrying on his spying activities. Somehow he was managing to get information from New York through to the Americans.

I wrote to him that night. Once a week he wrote to me from New York, and once a week I responded. Always he said he was fine. He walked about town freely, he said. He had even made friends with the British officers. He was a familiar figure around Manhattan's streets, and I was not to worry.

His letters kept me alive. Daniel had written that the army was leaving Morristown in May, but he could not tell me any more. In June David wrote from the hills above Boundbrook, saying they were well but he couldn't wait to get back into action again. Mama still did not know me as June and July passed. Becky and I had each staked out our own territory in and around the house, so we didn't have to converse often.

And then one day in early August, Canoe came home.

I was waiting on a customer in the shop when a shadow darkened the doorway. No sound accompanied it. I finished with my customer and looked up. "Canoe!"

Then, in a manner that was not at all proper, I ran across the floorboards and right into his arms. I had never done that before, but he picked me up and held me as Dan or David might have done, then set me down, smiling.

"So, you've grown up and taken your father's place. I always knew you would be the one to do it."

"Oh, Canoe, you know about Father's death!"

"We heard."

"Where is my grandfather? I do want to see him! Oh, Canoe, everything is awful! Mama is sick and I haven't heard from my brothers since June and John Reid is a prisoner and—"

"Not now," he hushed me. "Your grandfather is fine. He sent a wagonload of supplies. I must unload them."

Outside the shop I squealed in delight over the salt, molasses, pepper, bolts of linen, tobacco, needles and pins, and silk thread.

"Canoe, where did you get all of this?"

"I came by way of Philadelphia." That was all he would say.

He brought everything in the shop and put it on the shelves while I told him what had happened in their absence. "You must come in for supper, Canoe. Lucy will want to see you. We have plenty."

He shook his head and smiled. But he wouldn't look at me.

"You must, please! There's so much more I want to hear about Grandfather. I can't *believe* he's coming home! It'll be like having Father back again, almost! Oh, Canoe, please?"

He stood in the middle of the shop, his eyes sad, yet amused too. "Your sister..." he said.

"What of her?" But I knew. "Canoe, I'm mistress of this house. Dan has arranged for Grandfather Henshaw to send me an allowance to run it in his absence. I keep accounts of everything I do to show Dan. And of the shop, as well. Rebeckah is only visiting."

He looked at me hesitantly. "Oh, Canoe, come, please. It'll be like being with family again." I stopped, hoping I hadn't offended him.

I hadn't. "All right," he said, "for you."

I brought him into the kitchen, where he could have coffee. Lucy greeted him warmly, and then Becky appeared in the doorway, the baby in her arms. Canoe stood up respectfully and inclined his head.

"Hello, Canoe," she said curtly. "Jem, I'm desperately in need of help with the baby. I can't find that lazy Molly anywhere. Could I bother you for a minute?"

In the parlor she closed the door. "How dare you, Jemima Emerson! You know how I've always felt about him. Here I am, stuck in this ungodly town with a baby, trying to bring some decency back into this house, and you invite that..." She closed her eyes. "I want him out of the house immediately."

I felt as if she'd struck me. "Becky, he's practically family!"

"That's just *it!*"

She stared me down fiercely. And all the months of war and struggling, of facing Hessians and British, of seeing Father dead, of the work in the shop, all of it melted away. I was once again the little sister in the upstairs chamber being scolded for being unladylike.

"Please, Becky! He brought me supplies!"

"I don't care if he brought you four hundred Spanish dollars! I want him out!"

"I can't. I've invited him for supper."

"You can and you will. I have a baby in the house. Who knows what diseases he brings! Tell him the baby is running a fever. Tell him anything. But get him *out!*"

I was trembling when I left the parlor. But in the kitchen I found only Lucy, stirring the stew over the fire. "Where's Canoe?"

She just looked at me, and I knew he was gone. I went to bed early that night without supper, hating Becky more than I'd ever hated her. And hating myself more.


"Hello, Canoe."

He looked up from the harness he was fixing in the barn at Otter Hall. He was not surprised to see me, although it had taken me almost a week to get up the courage to ride over.

"It's hot to be out," he said.

"I should have come sooner. I couldn't get away."

"How are things going?"

"The supplies you brought me came from heaven."

He looked down at the harness. "Only Philadelphia. Hardly heaven."

"Have you heard from my grandfather?"

"He will be here by the end of October."

"I can't believe it. I've been so long without anyone in the family. Except Rebeckah."

He said nothing.

"Have you heard about Bennington, Vermont? We heard there was a British defeat up there."

"It's true," he said. "Captain Johnny Stark won a battle."

I sighed and looked out over the fields that lay in the

unreal blue-green haze of August. "The farm looks good, Canoe."

"You know better," he chided gently. "Most of the fields lie fallow. The repair work is piling up. But it will improve."

"Canoe, I'm sorry about last week."

"There is nothing to be sorry for."

"I should have stood up to Rebeckah. You had every right to stay."

His dark eyes smiled. "You've done enough standing up to people for a while, perhaps."

"No, Canoe. It never stops. It has nothing to do with war. It just never stops."

"You learned that too soon."

"Not soon enough."

"You've crowded too much into one year. Give yourself time."

"Canoe, I never wanted to hurt you. Grandfather will be furious with me when he finds out. And John Reid, why, he'd lecture me into next week if he knew. I've failed everybody."

"They don't have to know. And you haven't failed, because it didn't come from you."

"It did, because I did nothing. Because I didn't do what I should have done."

He was struggling with the harness. "You will when the time comes," he said.

"When will that be, Canoe? How will I know it? How can I be sure?"

"You will be," he said. "Now why don't you give that horse some water?"

# CHAPTER
## 33

By late August of 1777 all we knew was rumors about the war. I hadn't heard from my brothers since June. In mid-August John wrote from New York and said that he had been exchanged as a prisoner and freed from his parole. "I do not plan on returning to the American army yet," he wrote. "I have made such good friends here in Manhattan, I think I shall stay on awhile and rest. I have a bit of a cough."

Was he pretending to be sick in order to stay and gather information, or was he really ill? I had no way of knowing, and it maddened me.

In August Becky received a letter from Oliver saying that the British were pushing off in a fleet of over two hundred ships from Sandy Hook in New Jersey. If Becky knew where they were headed, she did not tell me. We didn't talk at all anymore.

Late in August Canoe had word that the Continental army was in Pennsylvania, heading toward a place called Brandywine. I didn't know what to believe anymore. And I was so exhausted I didn't care.

You couldn't believe anything you heard about the war, anyway. One minute we'd hear about a victory, the next a defeat. Becky let something out about Howe's junior officers being dissatisfied with the way he was running the campaign of 1777, since he seemed to be constantly stalling and letting the Americans elude him.

I was weary of it all. The war was practically ruining my father's shop. Canoe set off again the last day of August and brought me another wagonload of supplies. I didn't inquire where he'd gotten them. And I didn't invite him home for supper. But the supplies picked up my spirits the same way the pemmican used to when he gave it to me in the old days before I was grown up.

There comes a day each September when you wake up and know the summer is over and fall has arrived. The slant of the sun looks different and something is in the air—a coolness, a hint of frosty mornings to follow. I woke early on the morning of September 24 and reached for a warmer petticoat. In the kitchen I sat at the side of the table closest to the fire rereading the letter that had arrived from Dan the day before.

The news was not good. Washington's army had suffered a defeat at Brandywine on the 11th of September. But both Dan and David were still fine. I ate my breakfast and went to the shop.

Shortly after noon, when I'd finished the bit of stew left over from last night's supper, there came a knock on the shop door.

I sighed in exasperation. "Ought to make them wait," I mumbled, even as Father would have mumbled to himself. "A person can't even have a minute to have some nourishment."

But something about the shadow of the figure cast through the window caught my eye. It was not a civilian who had come to buy shoe buckles. It was a soldier. I shivered as I crossed the floorboards and fumbled with the door.

He just stood there. So did I, staring. I don't think I even blinked once. I'm sure he didn't. I went hot and then I went cold, then I closed my eyes for a moment, sure I would faint. Yes, it was a soldier, an officer in the Continental army.

"Well, aren't you going to invite me in, Jemima Emerson? Or have you forgotten your manners again?"

I backed into the shop. He followed, leaving the door ajar. Inside I stared at him, wide-eyed, unable to speak. I could see that he looked thinner and older.

He stood, looking very authoritative and handsome in his uniform, sizing me up. He walked around me as I stood in the middle of the shop, his boots clicking on the wooden floor. His eyes went over me from head to toe, and I flushed.

"Well, Jemima Emerson, you do look very grown up." He came full circle around me and stood surveying me sternly, his hands clasped behind his back.

"But you haven't curtsied. You do know how to curtsy. I've seen you do it. Can you do it for me?"

I was shaking so, I could barely manage it. But I did execute a fine curtsy, if I do say so myself. I raised my eyes to look at him.

"Your head and shoulders could be held a little higher, but it will do for now."

I straightened up. "How do you know so much about it, Mr. Reid?"

"I've been in the company of a few fine ladies in my time." A smile played about his lips, although he was doing his best to frown.

"I'm afraid I don't look anything like a lady today, sir."

"You look perfectly fine to me, Jemima Emerson." And then he smiled, gave a whoop, threw off his hat, and opened his arms. I ran to him. He embraced me and kissed me.

"John!"

Still kissing me, he turned and kicked the door shut with his foot.

# CHAPTER
## 34

At first I thought that John was just thinner than before and that he needed some home-cooked food. But after our first fierce embrace in the shop, he started to cough. And although he was sunburned from his travels, there were circles under his eyes.

"John, you *are* ill," I said.

"Just seeing you will make me well again."

"I thought when you wrote about having a cough, you were just pretending, so you could stay and gather information."

"I didn't have to pretend. But it came in handy, the cough. The British treated me beautifully, and I made friends with the officers and managed to send my superiors all kinds of information about British troop movements, shortages of supplies, and leading British officers."

"Why did you finally leave?"

"It was getting dangerous. My superiors knew I was sick and ordered me home for a rest. I've been traveling for a week, and it wore me down."

"And are you finished with all this now, Captain Reid?"

"For the time being. I was ordered to rest and recover. But I will go back. My services are needed." He coughed again.

"I think what is needed, John, is a good bowl of Lucy's soup. For your cough."

He ate the soup but not much else for supper. And I ate little more. I couldn't stop staring at him across the table. I couldn't believe he'd really come home. He looked around the dining room as if remembering it from some dream. He put up with Rebeckah's chatter, but always, it seemed, he was listening for something else. He had the soldier's trained eye and ear; nothing escaped him. And although I knew he was not feeling well, he did make a fine appearance at the table in a clean white shirt with a black silken stock under his collar.

"Stop staring at John," Rebeckah ordered. "You'll make him uncomfortable."

"How was the food when you were a prisoner, John?" I asked.

"Jemima!" Becky scolded. "Have you no feeling at all?"

"It's all right, Rebeckah," he said. "Jem should learn about such things."

"And you, I suppose, are still playing the tutor? Well, if you are, then you should tell her what it was like when Boston was evacuated a year ago last March. And how all those good Americans, whose only crime was being loyal to the King, were forced to leave their homes and possessions and sail for Halifax, Nova Scotia. Tell her how her aunt Grace was one of them. And you should let her know what it was like for them once they got to Halifax, with little shelter and food available."

"You were not there, Rebeckah," John said, "either for

the evacuation of Boston or the confusion in Halifax."

"Oliver was. And he wrote to me of it. What kind of a tutor are you if you only give her one side of the argument and withhold the full truth? Aunt Grace has now sailed for England, as have many of our good neighbors and friends who were Tories. Does she know that?"

"You are right, Rebeckah, I won't deny that," John said calmly. "We've lost many good Americans who had to flee because of their politics. And I shall educate Jemima about the matter when I have the time. But now I will answer her question. My provisions were sufficient, Jem. I wish I could say the same for other American soldiers who were prisoners in New York and weren't lucky enough to have privileges because they weren't officers. I visited some prisons and tried to help some of them, but the British didn't like my seeing all of that and they soon put a stop to it. I did find out that many American prisoners could have gotten out, had they agreed to enlist in the British army. Some did, with the plan to desert as soon as they could, but most of them died rather than defect to the enemy."

The candles were so bright in the room as I looked at him across the table. Or did it only seem so because of the tears in my eyes?

"This war has ruined the lives of many good people on both sides," John said. "But wars usually do that."

We took our coffee in the parlor. "You'll stay the night, John," I said. "Dan's room is empty." He reached out to take my hand as I went by his chair, and I could feel the warmth of his grasp.

"John, you're feverish."

"The fever always comes back at night," he said.

"You'll stay as long as need be," I amended. "You need to be looked after. Living alone, with no one to care for you, will only make you worse."

"I'll give you no argument tonight, Jemima," he said, leaning back and closing his eyes for a moment. "I'm pure exhausted. We can talk about it in the morning."

I had to take the cup from his hand, for he had the shivers then. Lucy had to help him up the stairs to bed.

I stayed in the parlor. The candles sputtered in the pewter holders. I would have given an arm if Mother or Father had been in the room so I could discuss John's homecoming and what it meant to me. I was unbearably happy, yet unbearably sad at the same time.

"Jemima."

Becky had left to see to the baby but now stood in the door of the parlor looking at me. "Jemima, I don't want to go through this with you again. I thought you had sense enough to spare us a second time."

What was she saying?

"I think sometimes you do things just to provoke me."

"Rebeckah, I don't know what you're talking about."

"Yes, you do. Don't pretend. You're no longer a child."

"That's news to me, coming from you. You always treat me like one."

"Perhaps because you insist on acting like one. How can you be anything but a thoughtless child when you invite him to stay here as long as need be?"

I felt every part of me come alert. "He's staying, Rebeckah. As long as need be."

"He has his own place."

"He's sick. He needs looking after and tending."

"And you're just the one to do it, I suppose. Wouldn't that look nice getting around town?"

"Becky, how can you? Are you afraid it wouldn't look

proper in front of your Tory lady friends who have nothing better to do than gossip? John is *sick!* There is nothing improper in this. Lucy is here with me. She'll do most of the tending."

"I have a baby in the house. We don't know what diseases he carries."

"Oh, Becky, don't say that again. You just don't want him here, admit it."

"All right, I will. Why should I have him under this roof? My husband is serving in the British army. I don't know if I'll ever see him again. And you invite a Continental soldier to stay in the house."

"This is *John*, Rebeckah. Our friend! He isn't just any soldier. And if he were just any soldier, I'd do it anyway. They starved for us; they died. You heard him."

"Fools."

"You *would* say that. What those men went through for us nobody can make up to them."

"I strongly suspect you're about to try."

I whirled on her. "Now what is *that* supposed to mean!"

"You've been making a fool of yourself over him all through supper. It isn't seemly, betrothed or not."

"Isn't *seemly!* I suppose it was seemly to have the Hessians and British in the house! You act as if the war never happened!"

"Oh, I know the war happened. But I feel it my responsibility, as your older sister, to keep this a decent Christian home."

"A decent Christian home is what it is. It's what Mama would do, taking John in."

"Mama! Don't talk to me of Mama or what she would do. I'm sick of your endless prattle about Mama. You're just like her, for heaven's sake!"

"And what's wrong with that?"

"You don't know?"

"I fail to see anything wrong with it, Rebeckah."

"You really don't know, do you? They never told you." And she laughed that bitter laugh of hers. "It's right you should know. It would take you down off that high horse of yours."

"If you have something to tell me, Becky, I think you ought to say it plain."

"All right, I will. She was responsible for Father's death."

A candle went out on the small round table in the corner. My mouth went dry. "What are you saying, Becky?"

"The truth. Father was killed, not for refusing to sign the loyalty oath to the King. Not even for serving on the Provincial Congress that voted for independence. He was killed because of those essays Mother was writing for the *Gazette*."

"You lie, Becky."

"Do I? The British killed him after they traced the letters to our name. The British, not the Hessians. They lured him out of town with that note to deliver supplies to the militia. That note came from the British, not Dickinson's militia. There were copies of Mama's essays pinned to his body when he was found in the shop the next day. They never told you, that's all."

"It isn't true."

"Isn't it? Ask the Moores. They know."

I sat down, trembling.

She went on. "Why do you think Mother went mad? It's from guilt. She can't forgive herself. She was told by Grandfather Henshaw to stop, but she wouldn't listen. Her precious principles were too important to her. She was a fool, getting involved in things a woman has no right getting involved in. And you're turning out to be just like her!"

"Stop it, Becky!"

"I won't! It's time you were told! You're spoiled. You always were. Mother and Father spoiled you. By the time they realized it, it was too late. They had to turn you over to John because they couldn't do anything with you anymore. There are plenty of things you don't know, Jemima."

My head was spinning. So this was what Mama's courage had wrought! What good was it all? I felt everything I believed in destroyed. No wonder Mama had gone daft. How did a person live with such a thing on her conscience?

Becky went to the door. "They should have told you a long time ago. I suggest you pray on it and act accordingly."

"Accordingly?" I looked at her.

"Learn from it. I also suggest you tell John in the morning to go home. There are indentured servants he can get to care for him. Or he can pay servants. He has money. If you don't, Jemima Emerson, within three days I will leave with the baby. Make your choice. Grow up, finally, or have us on your conscience."

She left the room.

I sat there a long time. The other candle in the corner went out. It was late, and the only light in the room came from the dying fire. It grew colder, but I still sat there, for the cold was mostly inside me.

# CHAPTER
## *35*

The next morning when I visited John he was sitting up in Daniel's bed, sipping something hot and steaming out of a mug. He looked rested but still weak. "Whatever it was that Lucy gave me last night helped. The fever is down."

"It was Mama's medicine." I felt a stab of remorse talking of her.

"It does me just as good to see you looking so bright and pretty this morning. Where are you off to so early?"

"To the Moores'. To see Mama."

"If I were up to it, I'd ride over with you on such a fine day. Look at that sky out there. It makes a man feel good to be alive."

"You aren't up to anything, John Reid. Lucy says you're to stay in bed today and rest or you won't be alive. We've sent for Dr. Cowell to come have a look at you."

"The devil you have. I won't have it."

"I'm afraid you must."

He took my hand, a glint of amusement in his eyes. "Is that how you take advantage of your tutor when he's had his horse shot from under him?"

"Yes."

"You always did want a way to get back at me, didn't you, Jemima Emerson?"

I kissed his forehead. "Yes, I have you now and you'll listen to me for a change." I smiled at him wishing I felt as sure as I looked walking out.


The Moores were in their barn. They came out when I rode into the barnyard. "That's a bit of hard riding for someone who should be in the shop this time of day," Mr. Moore said. "Is it not?"

I didn't have to pretend with the Moores, which made me glad. "I've come to see my mother," I said.

"Thee can see her anytime thee wishes," Ruth said.

I stood in the September sunlight looking at those two good, dear people who loved me as their own. "I have to ask you something, both of you."

They nodded and glanced at each other, waiting.

"Is it true about my mother and the letters? That my father was killed because of what she did?"

Mr. Moore looked at the ground. Ruth reached and touched my arm. "It is the truth," she said. "We hoped thee wouldn't have to hear it."

"Who told thee?" Mr. Moore asked.

"My sister, Rebeckah."

"I knew it was only a matter of time before that happened," he said. "We would have told thee, but we thought thee had enough to weigh down thy spirit."

I nodded. "I'd like to see my mother now, please."

"Would thee be telling thy mother what thee has learned?" Ruth asked.

"I would be. But it doesn't matter. She never pays attention to anything I say."

"Then why must thee tell her?" she insisted.

"I don't know. I just know I have to."

"Sometimes I think thy mother hears with her heart," she said. "Go. Thee knows where to find her."

"I don't know what to do with Becky, Mama. Things are just awful at home."

I sat at her feet on the braided rug in the sun-filled parlor. I had learned, over the long summer months, not to let her blank looks bother me. The Moores had encouraged me to talk to her and tell her what was going on at home. So I usually chatted with her as if she were perfectly normal.

"John Reid came home. You know I told you we were betrothed now. But he's sick. Lucy had to doctor him with your medicines. I told him he could stay at our place until he was well. And Rebeckah wants me to put him out."

She was sewing a petticoat, not looking at me.

"Mama, we had the most awful argument. She accused me of being like you. She said the trouble with you was that you couldn't give up your precious principles. And it was those principles that were the cause of Father's death."

I had never spoken to her of Father, not once in all my visits. But her face never changed, nor did she stop stiching.

"She said, Mama, that Father was killed because you wrote all those letters to the *Pennsylvania Gazette*. She said copies of the letters were . . . pinned to him when he was found."

There was silence in the room. Through the open window a bird sang and sounds of an autumn day drifted in the window. I heard a horse whinny from the barn.

"I always *wanted* to be like you, Mama. When I found out you were writing those essays, I wished I could be like you and do something to help the army. I thought you were so brave. But now Becky tells me it was stupid and that I'm the same way because I want to keep John in the house until he's well. She's given me a choice, Mama. She says that either John goes or she goes with the baby in three days. And I don't know what to do. I know they haven't anywhere to go. I'd be turning her out."

She was still sewing.

"Oh, Mama, I wish you could help me! I wish you could tell me what to do! I don't want to turn Becky out. But she's being unreasonable. And John is so sick. And if something happened to *him*, I'd die!"

I ran my finger along the braided rug. The sunlight was warm on my back. I felt better for having told her. It would be a long ride back on Bleu, and oh, I did feel so forlorn and tired. Wearily, I got to my feet. I leaned over and kissed her. "Well, Mama, thank you for listening. I must go now. That's a lovely petticoat you're making."

I walked to the door. "Goodbye Mama."

I was in the hall when I heard her voice. At first I thought I was dreaming it.

"Jem." So soft at first, and then louder. "Jemima."

I flew back into the room. She *knew* me! Never before had she called me by name!

"Yes, Mama?"

"Come, here, Jem, sit down."

I was shaking and I sank down like a sack of flour. "Yes, Mama, I'm here."

She kept right on stitching that petticoat. For a while she said nothing, and I thought I had lost her again. But soon she spoke.

"I sit here, day after day, Jem, and I think of what I did. And there are days when I know it was right. And days when I know it was wrong. What you must realize is that your heart breaks in life no matter what decision you make. Just make one. It's worse not to."

I looked into her eyes. "But, Mama, that's what you did."

"I know, child. I'm not here in this room because I'm not right in the head from what I did. I couldn't have you go away thinking that. I'm here because my heart is broken and I can't face the world. I can't do it anymore, Jem. I choose not to. The Moores have given me shelter until I feel I can face the world again. You mustn't tell anyone, Jem. I need more time."

"Oh, I won't, Mama. I promise."

"There are days I can't even talk to you. I knew who you were, Jem, right from the beginning. I just couldn't..." She started to cry.

Dear Lord, I hadn't wanted to make her cry. "Oh, don't cry, Mama, please!" I held her until she stopped.

When I had quieted her, she dried her eyes.

"I didn't want you to think I was out of my head from what I did. I couldn't have you afraid to do what you have to do."

"Thank you, Mama. I'm not afraid. But I don't know what to do."

She touched my face. "Yes, you do. Do what you know in your heart is right. Whatever decision you make, you'll feel bad. Life does that to us sometimes. Do what is right." She smiled. "You *are* a lot like me, Jemima. But you can learn from me. You can learn to live with your decision. That's what you must learn. If I can teach you that, I won't feel so bad."

I knew when I got home that day what I would do. As for whether I could live with my decision, well, that remained to be seen.

# CHAPTER
## *36*

Three days later my sister left our house for good. It was a beautiful day in late September when the carriage pulled up in front and she took her leave with the baby and the servant girl.

She would not say goodbye to me. The two days of her preparation to leave turned out to be a nightmare. I had been unable to sleep or eat. John Reid was still sick upstairs in Daniel's room. The doctor had come and gone and told us that sleep, care, and good food would put him on the mend again.

The house was so silent after they left. I couldn't believe that I had done what I had done or that she had carried out her threat and left.

So now I was indeed like Mama, with something on my conscience. For two days afterward I walked around like a ghost, doing my chores in the shop in a daze. I left my food untouched at the table. I snapped back at Lucy when she told me to eat, ordering her to leave me be.

On the third day I came in through the center hall after I had closed the shop.

"Jemima, come in here."

John was in Father's study, fully dressed. I was startled to see him downstairs, to hear his voice so firm and normal again. I stood in the doorway, staring.

"John, are you well enough to—"

"Come in here and close the door, please."

I closed it and stood against it. "What is it, John?"

He sat perched on the edge of Father's desk. "What's been going on, miss?"

"Why, nothing, John. Whatever do you mean?"

"Lucy tells me you're walking the house at night. You snap at her when she tells you to eat your food and order her to leave you alone. Now tell me, what is it?"

"I think Lucy must be imagining things."

"And I think you are lying to me."

"John, would I—"

"Yes, you would. Come here."

There was something of my old tutor in the way he said it. I raised my chin defiantly. "I was just about to clean up for supper."

"You were just about to come here."

There was no sense in upsetting him, since he'd been so ill lately. I went to him. I raised my eyes innocently, but he would have none of it.

"Now tell me what's going on?"

"Nothing, John. Heavens, can't a person be out of sorts?"

"Jemima Emerson, you may well lie to the saints on Judgment Day and get away with it, but I know you too well. What are you keeping from me?"

I smiled sweetly at him and fastened two buttons on his waistcoat.

"I quarreled with Rebeckah before she left to visit with her friend in New Brunswick."

"A quarrel with Rebeckah would bother you as much as a quarrel with a chipmunk. I see you are determined not to tell me."

"John, we women all have our little secrets. Won't you let me have mine?"

He moved away from the desk. He coughed. "I think that I shall move back to my quarters on King Street tomorrow."

"But why?" I felt alarmed.

"Jemima,"—he looked at me—"I am only a human being and so are you. It isn't good for us to be under the same roof like this until we marry. You may not admit it, but I will. I appreciate your hospitality, but it's time to go."

So that's what he thought was wrong, that I was languishing about because he was under the same roof with me! Well, let him think it, then. Better that than know the truth.

"But you can't go. You aren't well yet!"

"Oh, and you're telling me what I can and can't do now, miss?" He coughed again. "I'll be fine. Don't worry about me."

"You won't be fine! And I shall worry about you!" I stamped my foot and my lips trembled. Didn't he see? If he left now, my quarrel with Rebeckah would have been for nothing! I had stood up to her and done the right thing for the first time in my life. On my own. And for what?

For nothing. And I had Rebeckah on my conscience now, too. But I couldn't tell him that!

He stared at my outburst, open-mouthed. "I should be completely on my feet in a month, Jem," he said. "By that time your grandfather will be home. We can marry in October. What do you say?"

"If you leave, John Reid, you can marry yourself in October!" I burst into tears and ran from the room crying.

Of course it was childish and I knew it. And of course he left. He was too much of a man to allow a woman to tell him what he could and could not do. He stood in the hall the next morning and put his arm around me, humoring me like the child I still was.

"I'll be over tonight to court you properly, under Lucy's watchful eye," he teased.

"I may not be here tonight."

He kissed my forehead. "I wouldn't love you half as much if you hadn't such spirit, Jemima. But you do try my soul sometimes."

That afternoon Canoe came into the shop.

I had two customers. He waited in the background. Then, when they had left, he nodded at me.

"Beautiful weather," he said. "Blue skies and trees turning. A good day for a ride. Why don't you close up early?"

"Thank you, Canoe, but I don't feel up to it."

He sat down on a barrel. "I came to tell you something that might help you. Put the color back in your face, make you eat again."

"Why everyone is so concerned with my eating, I don't know."

He smiled. "Lucy told me of the argument with your sister."

"Lucy talks too much."

"The British have occupied Philadelphia."

I stared at him. "How would that make me happy, Canoe?"

"Four days ago now. Your sister left three days ago."

I stopped what I was doing and looked at him. He nodded. "She knew. She must have known since August they were heading there. All the officers knew. She got letters from him."

"You mean I didn't put her out? She had someplace to go?"

Again he nodded. "I have word from the driver of the carriage. She arrived there safely."

"Oh, Canoe, what would I do without you!"

"Now you can eat again and look healthy when your grandfather arrives."

I smiled at him through my tears. "It isn't that simple, Canoe. There's more to it. I was so worried about Rebeckah I wasn't eating, and John Reid thought it was because he was there under the same roof with me. Now he's left. And I quarreled with him because I thought I'd turned Rebeckah out in the cold for him. But I couldn't tell him that. Oh, Canoe, it's all so confused!"

He smiled. "It's always confused when there's love. He left because he has pride. Who wants a man without pride?"

"But he's still sick, Canoe. He won't cook properly for himself in those rooms of his. He has no one to care for him."

"We have room at Otter Hall."

"He wouldn't take your charity any more than he'd take mine."

"We also have a few Indian children running around there who need book learning."

"Oh, Canoe, that's a wonderful idea! But I couldn't ask him. He'd see through me in a minute."

"Then I will ask." He stood up. "I'll go there this afternoon and tell him your grandfather requests it while he's on leave, since he did such a fine job with you."

I blushed. "You've done much for me, Canoe."

He said nothing. I looked at him shyly. "Canoe, things are so mixed up in my head. I don't know if I'll ever get them straight again."

"Things are more straight in your head now than ever before," he said.

"I miss my father. There are days I don't think I can stand it."

He looked at me long and steadfastly. "Why do you think your grandfather sent me on ahead when he heard of his death?" he said.

Across the counter I looked at him. And it came to me then how stupid I was being. For he couldn't have said it plainer.

He was indeed my father's brother.

# *EPILOGUE*

Four years later, on October 22, a lone horseman rode into town and went straight to the Presbyterian church where everyone gathered to hear news of the war.

People were running out of houses and shops and heading in the direction of the church. It was then that I heard the cry taken up by one, then the other and passed around.

"Yorktown!"

I stood on the steps of the shop. "What is it? What's happened?"

A young indentured servant boy came flying out of the Black Horse Tavern. "The war is over! The British surrendered at Yorktown!"

Yorktown. I knew the name, for John had written to me of such a place and all the other important places in his letters, which he sent in invisible ink.

John and I had married when my grandfather Emerson came home in the fall of 1777. John left to rejoin the army in December, deliberately had himself captured again, and was held prisoner in Philadelphia until June of 1778 when the British evacuated that town.

The British shipped him to New York. It was then that I started getting the letters in invisible ink. One day a package was sent to me with a curious-looking chemical in it, with the message to keep it and rub it over the entire next letter that came. When I did, another message became clear, in between the lines!

That was how I knew what John was up to and how I kept from going mad in the next three years. For a handsome sum he was persuaded to defect to the British in New York, for his reputation as a journalist was well known. And so, once again, he was writing for the *New York Gazette*, the infamous Tory newspaper. He would frequent coffeehouses where the British went, pick up information, and get it out to the Americans.

He never met Washington, although his maps, sketches, and reports went directly to Washington himself. It would have been too dangerous for a spy to have come in contact with him.

Until the end of the war he and others like him kept up the flow of information—news of the arrival of British ships, British losses in battles, and the doings of British generals.

"Yorktown!" The cry was taken up by man, woman, and child as they rushed past me down the street. I stood there on the steps of Father's shop. Yorktown, Brandywine, Valley Forge, Monmouth Courthouse, Savannah, Guilford Courthouse, Cowpens. I knew all the names.

John was still tutoring me.

The tears came down my face as I stood there. The war was over! How long ago it was when it started! I had been a little girl of fifteen, running off on my tutor, arguing with Lucy, upsetting Mama, provoking Father, learning to shoot a musket on a hill in town.

I heard more names as the crowd went by. The French.

Rochambeau. Cornwallis. De Grasse and a battle at sea. Washington. The long siege over at Yorktown. Cornwallis. Beaten to the sea.

Two weeks later, in mid-November, I came in from the shop after closing. It was dark outside and the candles in the hallway welcomed me. As I closed the door I saw Lucy standing at the end of the hall.

"What is it, Lucy? In heaven's name, what's the matter?" She looked as if she had just taken leave of her senses.

She raised her hands in the air, opened her mouth, but did not speak. A stab of fear went through me. Dear God, what now? Was there bad news about Daniel? David? John?

"Jemima Emerson, will you come in here, please?"

I froze in my tracks, hearing his voice from Father's study. I flew down the hall and stood there. For a moment neither one of us moved. He was wearing his American uniform again, his coat open, his hat on the desk.

I screamed, threw my cloak off, and ran to him. He caught me in his arms and kissed me. I was crying and kissing him all at once.

"Barbarians come into a room with such an entrance, Jemima Reid," he said.

"I don't care."

"Have I taught you nothing?"

I clung to him. "It looks, sir, as if you will have to teach me all over again."

The cold November wind whipped through the church-yard of St. Michael's. I stood there with Dan and Betsy Moore and John and Cornelius and Lucy. Dan was a major. He'd proven himself at Valley Forge, Monmouth, and the whole southern campaign. He stood next to me. In his hand he held the wrinkled flag that he had brought from York-town. Its red and blue were faded and it was torn. He smiled at me, then he and John fastened it onto the make-shift pole and planted it in the ground over Father's grave.

"It's too bad David couldn't be buried here, too," I said.

David had been killed at Yorktown, storming a re-doubt, something he wasn't ordered to do. David, who always tried to please Father, killed himself in a final attempt to avenge Father's death. He was buried somewhere in Virginia.

Grandfather Henshaw, because he was a Tory, had to leave the country for Canada, and Becky went with him to stay until she could go back to England with her husband.

Dan and Cornelius were home for only two days while the army passed through Trenton on its way north. The war was over, but they were not yet discharged.

The night before, after supper, Dan had summoned John and me into the parlor and showed us the flag and asked us to come to the churchyard with him.

"Do you think Mother will want to come?" he asked me.

Dan was twenty-six, a full-fledged man. He and Betsy would marry when he was discharged and make Father's house their home. He asked John and me to stay in the house, however, and keep things going until that time came, even though John was purchasing Major Barnes's house for us on Queen Street.

I was twenty-one. "No, Dan, I don't think Mother should come. It wouldn't do her any good. She'll never be the same. You've only been home a day, so you can't tell. She's never talked about the war in the last three years since she's been home again. Or even gone into Father's shop."

"It's the only way she could live with it, Jem," John said.

Dan nodded. I could see the hint of tears in his eyes. "You've done such an excellent job with her, Jem, and with the house and the shop, that I want to give you the shop. Lord knows I've no need for it. I'll be getting back to my books and my law."

"Daniel Emerson, you may have fought for freedom, but don't you know? Married women can't own property. Things have changed, but not that much!"

"Why, then"—he smiled—"that's a war you'll have to fight out with your husband, madam. Knowing you, I'm sure you'll get the best of the arrangement after all."

From the corner of my eye I saw John move away from me in the cemetery and incline his head toward the others. Leave it to John to know I wanted to be alone. But now that I was alone, my heart was so full I could barely breathe.

"The flag Dan brought is beautiful, Father. You'd like it. Oh, it's kind of faded and there's a tear in one place, but Dan said you wouldn't mind that. I remember the day you said you wished we had one to fly when the British came to town.

"If I had a flag to give you, it would look just like this one, faded and wrinkled, with a tear in it. Somehow I do feel as if I have one for you, even though mine can't be seen.

"It's what I've become that I can give you, Father. I've grown up, at last. Oh, it was a long time coming. But I've learned some of the things finally, that you and Mama were always trying to tell me.

"For one thing I've learned that doing what you think is right doesn't always make you feel good. For another, I've learned that sometimes you just have to keep on going when you want to do nothing but drop. And that just doing the everyday things, like keeping a shop running or getting up every morning, will keep the world going until things can straighten out again. And doing those things right every day soon becomes more important than the more pressing issues of the time.

"Civility, you used to say, and an army coming through shouldn't make any difference.

"Lord, Father, I've gone and married John Reid. Did you ever think I'd do such a thing? Of course you did! You and Mama were forever talking him up to me. You wanted our marriage right from the beginning, didn't you?

"I only wish you could be here to see our children someday when we have them, and help us teach them to handle this liberty we've won for ourselves. Nobody knows what it really means yet. We're just glad the war is over and all the killing is done with.

"I'm going to leave now. The sun is nice here, and I suppose St. Michael's will be opening again soon. Reverend Panton's house was destroyed. By the British! John Fitch's shop was burned to the ground. The bell of St. Michael's was carried off, twenty-four pews were destroyed, and twelve common seats were ruined. The pulpit and reading desk are damaged, but everything will be fixed again.

"Oh, Lord, Father, freedom's nice. But sometimes I ache wishing we could all go back to the way things were before the war, when we were together.

"Well, I have to go now. They're waiting for me by the gate."

# *AUTHOR'S NOTE*

The thirteen colonies in North America were only a part of the British possessions scattered throughout the world, and before 1763 they were not considered the most valuable part. Up until the French and Indian War (1754–1763), the thirteen colonies were left, within broad limits, to pursue their own interests and were able to assert fairly extensive rights of self-government.

After winning the French and Indian War in North America, England was left with the problem of defending the new territory it had acquired from the French and the staggering burden of the war debt. To solve these problems, King George the Third of England took several courses of action. He established a western boundary line along the Allegheny Mountains beyond which the colonists could not settle. He stationed British soldiers in America to enforce this Proclamation Line and to keep the Indians at peace, and he also passed the Stamp Act in 1765, imposing a tax on most paper items purchased by the colonists. But the colonists rejected this tax on the grounds that they, as Americans, possessed all the rights of English subjects, most especially the right to be taxed only by their own representatives.

In various places, like Boston, mob riots broke out and eventually the Stamp Act was repealed in 1766, but only after England passed the Declaratory Act, which gave the English Parliament the authority to make any and all kinds of laws to keep control over the colonists. But the colonists were not about to accept this parliamentary authority either. It was seen as a threat to their self-government. The Americans had gained a new attitude about themselves after the French and Indian War. They were more self-confident in their military prowess and held contempt for the British soldiers and officers with whom they did not get along during the war. With the French threat mostly gone, the colonists believed they could take care of themselves and needed less guidance and rule from England. They were a strong people who had made their way in a wild land, and the very act of taming that land gave them a self-reliance the Europeans did not have. They believed that the laws of nature and God justified them in resisting any intrusion on their rights.

Between 1763 and 1775, England passed the Sugar Act (1764) and the Townshend duties (1767), which required the colonists to pay taxes on certain items. Again, the colonists opposed these taxes and, except for a tax on tea, all were repealed. Mob violence again erupted, and in March 1770, Americans confronted British troops in what became known as the Boston Massacre. In December 1773, Americans dressed as Indians threw tea into the water from British ships in Boston Harbor to protest the tea tax in what has come to be called the Boston Tea Party.

The English Parliament then passed the Coercive Acts of 1774 to punish the colonists. It was during this year that the colonists began to unite to resist England. The Continental Congress, a body of learned men representing each colony, met in sessions in Philadelphia to unite the colonies and to discuss their problems. In September of 1774, the Continental Congress sent a list of colonial grievances to King George. They also agreed not to buy any more goods from England and made military preparations for defense against attack by British troops.

The colonists stopped drinking tea and started wearing homespun clothing rather than import these and many other products from the mother country. Then, in the early months of 1775, people in Massachusetts began to gather arms and ammunition and to train local men to fight. The British troops in Boston under General Thomas Gage, aware of this activity, were sent on April 18 to capture a large supply of ammunition in Concord and arrest the Rebel leaders, Sam Adams and John Hancock. On April 19, 1775, the first shots of the War for Independence were fired on Lexington Green.

After the battles of Lexington and Concord in April 1775, the colonial armed forces took the offensive. The Americans circled and besieged the British army in Boston and, though suffering severe casualties in the Battle of Bunker Hill on June 17, 1775, inflicted heavier losses on the British. The Americans penned the British in Boston all that summer, fall, and winter. Food in Boston became scarce, sickness threatened to spread, and Loyalists (Americans loyal to King George) streamed into Boston from the surrounding areas. The Patriots (those fighting for independence) were not tolerant of fellow Americans who were loyal to the King so those Loyalists or Tories sought protection from the British in America.

Then, in March of 1776, General George Washington, commander in chief of the American army, fortified Dorchester Heights above Boston with cannon brought down from Fort Ticonderoga through the winter snow by Colonel Henry Knox. Rather than fight Washington, the British general Sir William Howe sailed away to Halifax, Nova Scotia, but he returned to the American colonies in July of 1776.

Howe's redcoat army consisted of 32,000 soldiers. General Washington's Continental army (the regular American army formed under the Continental Congress) had about

19,000 men. Washington's brave but poorly trained soldiers met defeat at the Battle of Long Island in August, the Battle of Harlem Heights in September, and the Battle of White Plains in October. After pushing the Continentals out of New York City and into North Jersey, the British attacked and captured two important American forts, Washington and Lee, on the Hudson.

It was now November, and Washington's army began its famous retreat through New Jersey. New York City was lost and not a single battle had been won since the Continental army was established in July, 1775. The British captured 2,900 Americans when they took Fort Washington. A large amount of much-needed artillery, equipment, and supplies was lost to the enemy at Fort Lee, the weather was damp and cold with fog and heavy rains, and now it seemed that the small band of 3,000 men under Washington, which was plagued with desertion, would have to yield the colony of New Jersey to the enemy. This they did on December 7–8, 1776.

Having missed the chance to capture and destroy Washington's force, General Howe and Lord Charles Cornwallis and the British army settled down for the winter in New Jersey. Posts were established at Bordentown, Penny Town (Pennington), Trenton, Princeton, and New Brunswick. General Howe announced an offer of pardon to those Americans who would take an oath of loyalty to the king, and many did.

Meanwhile, Washington's army stood on the Pennsylvania side of the Delaware River, freezing and waiting. Many men were sick, and all were poorly clothed. Enlistments would be up on December 31. Then there would no longer be an army unless morale and spirits could be raised. Only a victory would give life to the dying cause. Washington knew this and formed a plan to cross the ice-clogged Delaware River on Christmas and attack and take the town of Trenton. He conferred with his officers—Generals Sullivan, Mercer, Lord Stirling, and St. Clair, Major General

Greene, Colonel Knox and others. The plan to take Trenton was kept secret, even from the enlisted men who were about to take part in the crossing. Washington's army in Pennsylvania was joined by Continental troops who had been left in New York before the retreat. New Jersey militia (citizen-soldiers who fought and went home after fighting) harassed the British and Hessians (paid German soldiers fighting for King George) at the Trenton outposts every chance they got.

"I think the game is pretty near up," Washington wrote to his brother. But he did not for a moment weaken in his high resolve. Aided by secret information given to him by spies, Washington did not hesitate to take the gamble and attack Trenton. But first he had to cross the icy Delaware River, under cover of darkness, with 2,400 men and horses and artillery.

Safe in their winter quarters in Trenton, where they were celebrating Christmas, the Hessians, under the command of Colonel Johann Gottlieb Rall, did not expect the attack. The crossing took longer than planned because of the weather. It was nearly four o'clock in the morning of December 26 before Washington's army was across the Delaware and the march on Trenton could begin.

This, then, is the historical background for my story. I have done my utmost to preserve the historical integrity of the Revolutionary era. During the Hessian occupation of Trenton in 1776, for example, no Americans were killed. In keeping with this fact, I have one American in my fictional family who is killed, lured out of town by the British. I have been careful not to tamper with the character of General Washington or any other important historical figure of the day. In doing research, I found that information about townspeople who stayed in Trenton at the time of the battle is scarce. It took me three months of research to find personal papers of a family who stayed in Trenton at the time of the battle.

The Emerson family is fictional, as are the Moores, John Reid, grandfathers Emerson and Henshaw, Canoe, Lucy, and Cornelius. But there were Indians living in Trenton at the time as well as black slaves and certainly many Quakers. Reverend Panton of St. Michael's and Reverend Spencer of the First Presbyterian, John Barnes, Stacy Potts, Isaac Allen, Daniel Coxe, Sam Henry, Dr. William Bryant, and others all actually lived in Trenton at the time, as did Sam Tucker, head of the Provincial Congress (the congress the colony of New Jersey organized to assume the power of government for those who wanted independence, since the New Jersey Assembly, under Royal Governor William Franklin, was split over the issue).

John Fitch, a staunch Patriot in Trenton, was later credited as being one of the inventors of the steamboat. Captain Andrew Bygrave and Lieutenant Colonel William Harcourt of the 16th Light Dragoons were two of twenty British in town at the time. I have used them in the book for my own purposes.

The Battle of Trenton marked an important turning point in the American Revolution. In one brilliant stroke, General Washington turned a ragtag, starving, ill-dressed, and defeated band of Rebels into a victorious army that defeated the most powerful army in the world—the British and their Hessian mercenaries. It brought confidence back to the cause for independence. Hundreds of men rallied to join Washington's ranks, and many people contributed much-needed money. It revived the hopes of not only the American people, but of the army itself and the Continental Congress. It proved that Washington was more than a capable commander in chief, that more victories were possible in the future, and that the American army need never again apologize for not being able to stand up against a foreign power.

Ann Rinaldi
*September 15, 1985*

# *ACKNOWLEDGMENTS*

This book could not have reached completion without the support, friendship, and inspiration of many good people, some of whom I would like to thank here.

For their kindness and assistance, the staffs of both the Academy Street and Cadwalader branches of the Trenton Public Library. For continued encouragement and friendship, the staff of Washington Crossing State Park, Washington Crossing, Pa., where my family and I have been taking part in the Crossing since 1976; Kels Swan, curator of Washington Crossing State Park, Titusville, N.J.; the good people at Historic Summerseat in Morrisville, Pa.; Cynthia Koch, Director, and the staff of the Old Barracks Museum in Trenton; Charlotte Gulliver, curator of the Trent House, Trenton; Mary Alice Quigley of the New Jersey Historical Commission; Loretta Brennan of the New Jersey School Boards Association, for her invaluable support when I needed it most; the Staff of Dey Mansion in Wayne, N.J., and the Passaic County Park Commission, for allowing us to use the mansion for artwork for the cover since this is the house I had in mind for the Emerson family in my book; Emil Slaboda, editor of *The Trentonian* newspaper, for sending me on a story about the 200th anniversary of the crossing of the Delaware in 1976; Reverend John Wiley Nelson of the First Presbyterian Church, whose sermon about the concept of freedom in 1776 made me decide to set my story in Trenton; and Reverend Raul Mattei of St. Michael's Episcopal Church, where so many prominent citizens of Trenton from 1776 are buried in the historic cemetery.

Thanks also to the men, women, and children of the Brigade of the American Revolution with whom I have traveled from Georgia to Canada to reenact America's struggle for independence; in particular the Egg Harbor Guard and the Bergen County Militia, for providing the color, drama, and pageantry that gave me a feeling for the era; my writer friends Susan Elizabeth Phillips, Gina Cascone, Barbara Cohen, Judith Gorog, and Avi Wortis (who said write it), and historian and fellow journalist Bill Dwyer, for their continued patience, listening, and advice; my husband, Ron, for his devotion and understanding; my daughter, Marcella, for posing as Jem for the book cover and for her services as courier with the manuscript on her many trips to New York City; my son, Ron, not only for posing as John Reid for the cover, but also for his rendering of maps for the book, the use of his extensive library on the American Revolution, for continually lending his historical expertise, and for being the original catalyst who encouraged my interest in our country's history.

Last and wholeheartedly, I thank my editor, Margery Cuyler, and John Briggs, President of Holiday House, Inc., for believing in this book when nobody else in the publishing world would.

Ann Rinaldi
*September 15, 1985*

# BIBLIOGRAPHY

A historical novel like this one would be impossible to write if one could not refer to the scholarly writings of men and women who have researched the period. Because I love American history, I have read widely about the eighteenth century in this country. That reading, combined with the years I spent reenacting the encampments and battles of the War for Independence with the Brigade of the American Revolution, gave me a fundamental knowledge of the era. The books and original papers I used for reference for this work, the ones I found most useful, are listed below, with many thanks to the authors who so painstakingly did the original research.

## Original Papers

*The Papers of Jemima Condict, 1771–1778:* Courtesy of the New Jersey Historical Society, Newark, N.J.

*A Grandmother's Recollection of Old Revolutionary Days: Recollections of Martha Reed Shannon, as Recorded by Her Granddaughter, Susan Pindar Embury, in 1875:* Courtesy of the Rare Books and Manuscripts Department, Firestone Library, Princeton, N. J.

"Trenton, New Jersey 1719–1779: A Study of Community Growth and Organization" by Stephanie Smith Toothman. Ph.D. dissertation, University of Pennsylvania, 1977. Courtesy of the Academy Street Branch of the Trenton Public Library.

## Books

Bakeless, Katherine, and John Bakeless. *Spies of the Revolution*. New York: Scholastic Book Services, 1973.

Bill, Alfred Hoyt. *New Jersey and the Revolutionary War*. New Brunswick, N. J.: Rutgers University Press, 1964.

Bowman, Larry G. *Captive Americans: Prisoners during the American Revolution*. Athens, Ohio: Ohio University Press, 1976.

Connors, Richard J. *The Constitution of 1776*. Trenton: New Jersey Historical Commission, 1975.

Cunliffe, Marcus. *George Washington, Man and Monument*. New York and Ontario: New American Library, 1958.

De Pauw, Linda Grant. *Founding Mothers: Women of America in the Revolutionary Era*. Boston: Houghton Mifflin Co., 1975.

De Pauw, Linda Grant, and Conover Hunt. *Remember the Ladies*. New York: Viking Press in association with the Pilgrim Society, 1976.

Gruber, Ira D. *The Howe Brothers and the American Revolution*. New York: W. W. Norton, 1972.

Ketchum, Richard M. *The World of George Washington*. New York: American Heritage Publishing Co., 1974.

Kull, Irving S., and Nell M. Kull. *A Short Chronology of American History, 1492–1950*. New Brunswick, N.J.: Rutgers University Press, 1952.

Lender, Mark E. and Joseph Kirby Martin. *Citizen Soldier, the Revolutionary War Journal of Joseph Bloomfield*, Newark, N.J.: The New Jersey Historical Society, 1982.

Myers, Albert Cook, ed. *Sally Wister's Journal: Eyewitness Accounts of the American Revolution*. New York: New York Times and Arno Press, 1969 (Philadelphia: Ferris and Leach Publishers, 1902).

Neuenschwander, John A. *The Middle Colonies and the Coming of the American Revolution*. Port Washington, N.Y.: National University Publications, Kennikat Press, 1973.

Royster, Charles. *A Revolutionary People at War: The Continental Army and the American Character, 1775–1783*. New York and London: W. W. Norton, 1975.

Seely, Rebecca, and Carey Roberts. *Tidewater Dynasty: A Biographical Novel of the Lees of Stratford Hall*. New York: Harcourt Brace Jovanovich, 1981.

Smith, Samuel Stelle. *The Battle of Trenton*. Monmouth Beach, N.J.: Philip Freneau Press, 1965.

Stone, Irving. *Those Who Love: A Biographical Novel of Abigail and John Adams*. New York: New American Library, 1965.

Stryker, William S. *The Battles of Trenton and Princeton*. Boston and New York: Houghton Mifflin Co., 1898. Reprint, Spartanburg, S.C.: Reprint Co., 1967.

Stryker, William S. *Trenton, One Hundred Years Ago*. MacCrellish and Quigley, 1878; Narr, Day, and Narr, 1893.

Trenton Historical Society, *A History of Trenton, 1679-1929*. Princeton, N.J.: Princeton University Press, 1929.